The Type-A Guide to Dinner Parties

A Sunset Ridge Cozy Mystery, Volume 2

Elizabeth Spann Craig

Published by Elizabeth Spann Craig, 2024.

This is a work of fiction. Similarities to real people, places, or events are entirely coincidental.

THE TYPE-A GUIDE TO DINNER PARTIES

First edition. November 19, 2024.

Written by Elizabeth Spann Craig.

Thanks to Janet and Shelly for your ideas and help!

Chapter One

S am Prescott stood in her kitchen, surrounded by an arsenal of party supplies that would make a military quartermaster envious. She checked her lists one more time, her pen hovering over the paper like a hummingbird, unsure where to land. The problem was, everything was already checked off and struck through. Yet somehow, she still didn't feel prepared for the dinner party she was giving.

"There's nothing else to do, Arlo," she said to her small rescue dog, who was watching her with an expression that seemed to say, 'You know this is overkill, right?' "We'll just have to make a new list."

Arlo's tail thumped against the floor, either in agreement or a desperate attempt to distract her from list-making madness.

As Sam scribbled furiously, her phone buzzed with yet another text message. She loved that everyone wanted to contribute, but at this point—mere minutes before the dinner party was to begin—offers of homemade potato salad and Great-Aunt Edna's secret recipe fruitcake were about as welcome as a tornado at a kite festival.

"Wine," she muttered, tapping out a quick response. "Just bring wine. We can never have too much wine tonight." She paused, realizing how that sounded. "Not that we're planning on drowning our sorrows or anything, Arlo. It's going to be a perfectly lovely evening."

Arlo tilted his head, unconvinced.

The truth was, Sam's brain wasn't exactly cooperating. In the past, hosting dinner parties had been as effortless as breathing. She could pull something like this together in her sleep. But things were different now. For one, she was newly divorced, and her ex-husband was in prison. It turned out that added a certain *je ne sais quoi* to party planning that Emily Post had never covered.

For weeks after Chad's arrest, it seemed like everyone in the neighborhood had brought casseroles. Sam suspected it was equal parts sympathy and curiosity.

Now, she was trying to move past all that and have a fresh start. She and Arlo would host a dinner party with a nice representation of guests from the neighborhood. Maybe it would stop the whispers, the sidelong glances, the conversations that mysteriously halted when she entered the room. She'd wanted to keep things intimate, though, and not take on too much for the night. She'd invited her friend Olivia, her husband, and Olivia's brother. She'd invited the new couple in the neighborhood. And Mandy and Alfred, who'd been so lovely and generous to her lately.

Of course, there was also the matter of Nora. Sam hadn't invited her, citing space concerns—the dining room table only held so many, after all. But deep down, she knew it was because

Nora was about as subtle as a foghorn and twice as loud. The last thing this delicate social situation needed was Nora's particular brand of "help."

The phone rang, startling Sam out of her thoughts. "Hello?"

"It's Olivia," came the chipper voice on the other end. "I wanted to see if I could help out."

It was a nice offer, but the idea of delegating even the smallest task made Sam's type-A personality break out in hives. "I think I've got it all under control, but thanks! You're sweet to call."

"I'll come early and help with the final bits and pieces," Olivia persisted. Before Sam could protest, she added, "So, who all is coming tonight?"

Sam's mind immediately shifted to the guest list, momentarily forgetting about Olivia's offer to help. "Well, we have you and Dom, Vanessa and Derek Martin, your brother Jason, and Mandy and Alfred."

"So that makes eight of us, counting you. That's pretty ambitious for a party."

"Is it?" Sam frowned. "I've hosted more in the past."

"For dinner? Or for drinks?"

"Oh." Sam paused. "You're right. It was for cocktails. Easier setup altogether."

There was a moment of silence before Olivia spoke again. "I noticed Nora's not on the list."

"Limited space, you know."

"Mm-hmm," Olivia hummed, unconvinced. "Are you sure that's the only reason? Or is it because she's a nosy old windbag with all the tact of a bull in a china shop?"

"Nora's . . . fine," Sam said diplomatically. "She has a talent for getting on people's bad sides."

"That's a generous way to put it," Olivia laughed. "You were smart not to invite her, Sam. You didn't need that kind of drama at your dinner party." She paused. "How are you doing, by the way?"

The unspoken questions hung in the air. Are you okay hosting a party without your husband? Are you okay that your husband is in prison right now? But Sam sidestepped them entirely. "Oh, doing well. Everything's going smoothly. I'm waiting for my meringues to rise. Hopefully they'll cooperate soon."

"All right, well, I'll let you go. I'll be there at quarter till."

Before Sam could protest, Olivia had hung up. She looked at Arlo, who wagged his tail expectantly. "Yes, I know you like Olivia. I'm sure you'll love seeing her here early." She sighed. "I suppose I should come up with something for her to do."

Arlo's tail wagged harder, as if in agreement.

"The flowers, maybe? Olivia seems like she'd enjoy arranging them."

Arlo cocked his head to the side, giving her a quizzical look.

"Oh, I've already arranged them into a bouquet, of course. They're in the fridge. But she can put them in one of the vases." Sam nodded decisively and pulled out a couple of options. "There. That's delegating, right?"

Arlo sneezed, which Sam chose to interpret as canine approval.

As she put the finishing touches on the hors d'oeuvres, Sam couldn't shake the feeling that, despite all her planning, something was bound to go awry. It was as if the universe had a surprise guest of its own lurking in the wings.

"Well, Arlo," she said, straightening her dress and giving her loyal companion a scratch behind the ears, "whatever happens, at least we'll have plenty of wine."

It felt like only a few minutes before the doorbell rang. Sam assumed Olivia would come by herself to set up, but instead she'd come with her husband, Dom, and her brother, Jason. Sam stifled a sigh. Now entertaining would factor into the equation. Or would it? She looked curiously at the three of them. Olivia seemed very stressed out and was avoiding eye contact. Jason's face was flushed, as if he'd been engaged in an argument. And Dom was vacillating between looking sulky and aggressive. Sam could smell liquor coming from both Dom's and Jason's directions. It looked as if there might have been some pre-party drinking going on. Arlo was watching them thoughtfully from across the room. Smart dog to stay back and just observe.

"Hi there!" said Sam, a welcoming smile spreading across her face. She pretended she could overlook the obvious mood surrounding the three. "Thanks so much for coming."

"Thanks for having us," said Dom smoothly. He proffered the bottle of wine he'd brought, which was a very expensive vintage.

"I'll open it," said his wife, taking it from him and moving swiftly into the kitchen.

Sam smiled at Dom and Jason. "I set up my office as a temporary coat closet. It's right over there."

By the time Dom and Jason returned, they were already in a heated argument, one which Sam couldn't follow. She was a little at a loss. She needed to be pulling appetizers and other food out of the oven, but had the feeling there would be an icy silence between the two men if she left them. Or, even worse, a continuation of the ugly argument. Since she gathered the issue might be Dom, not Jason, she said, "Jason, can you give me a hand in the kitchen? Dom, feel free to pour yourself a drink—the bar is over there."

Jason followed her into the kitchen, where Olivia was hovering. Sam had no idea what was going on, but they both seemed jumpy. She said, "Olivia, could you arrange some flowers in one of these vases? They're in the fridge." She paused, trying to come up with something for Jason to do. "And Jason, could you check and see what the conditions are like out on the terrace? I'd love us to sit out there for drinks or dessert, but I'm not sure how windy it is."

Jason headed out the door with a look of relief. Olivia cast an apologetic glance at Sam. "Dom's in a real mood tonight," she said in a low voice. "I'm so sorry. He has no business being at anybody's dinner party. And you've done such an amazing job making everything perfect."

"There's nothing to be sorry about," said Sam immediately. "We have no control over other people. If we did, I'm pretty sure Chad wouldn't be in prison right now."

Olivia gave a gasping laugh. "I didn't think of it that way."

Sam said in a low voice, "Hey, are you okay?" She hated the idea that Olivia was having to deal with any sort of verbal or physical abuse. She definitely didn't have any proof of that, but sometimes she got an uncomfortable feeling in her gut.

Olivia nodded quickly. "Absolutely. Dom is having a rough day, that's all."

Sam gave her a smile, and they chatted about lighter topics as Olivia arranged the flowers. But Sam was worried about Olivia. She thought she was making excuses for Dom. What if this wasn't an example of Dom having a rough day, but an example of Dom *every* day? And Sam really liked Olivia. It was the reason she was having them over for dinner.

Jason came back inside. "It's pretty blustery out there, Sam. Maybe if we all bundled up?"

Sam made a face. "Nope! Blustery wasn't what I had in mind. It's okay—we'll go out on the terrace another time when the weather is a little better. November isn't exactly the perfect month for being outside, anyway."

She could tell Jason didn't want to leave the kitchen to join Dom in the living room. Sam wondered again how much Dom had been drinking. She'd had the impression maybe he'd already been imbibing before he came over, and he'd likely had more since arriving. The doorbell chimed, its melodic tone echoing through the house. Then there was a voice calling, "Yoo-hoo! Sam?"

Sam grinned at hearing Mandy's voice. She hurried over to greet them, seeing their faces wreathed in warm smiles. Jason followed her, seeming relieved to have more of a buffer between him and Dom. Olivia trailed behind, clutching the vase of flowers. Mandy held a colorful casserole dish, while Alfred held a bottle of wine.

"Welcome!" Sam said, stepping aside to let them in. "I'm so glad you could make it."

"Wouldn't miss it for the world," Alfred rumbled good-naturedly, his eyes crinkling at the corners. "Something smells fantastic in here."

As they entered, Sam noticed Mandy's eyes darting around, taking in the decor. "Oh, Sam," she breathed, "your home is always so lovely. Those curtains in the living room—are they new?"

"Thanks! I just put them up last week. I'm still getting used to them myself."

She led them into the room, where Arlo greeted them with an enthusiastic tail wag. Alfred immediately crouched down to give the little dog a scratch behind the ears.

"Can I get you something to drink?" Sam offered, ever the attentive hostess. "I've got that pinot noir you like, Mandy, or there's a chardonnay if you prefer white."

"The pinot sounds perfect," Mandy said. She handed the casserole dish to Sam, suddenly looking a little shy. "I brought my green bean casserole you mentioned enjoying at the last neighborhood do. I hope that's okay?"

"More than okay," Sam assured her, heading to the kitchen to fetch the wine and put the casserole with the other dishes. "It'll go wonderfully with the roast."

As she poured the wine, she could hear Alfred and Mandy chatting quietly with Olivia in the living room, their voices a comforting murmur. The sound warmed her heart; this was exactly what she'd hoped for when planning this dinner party. A chance for neighbors to come together and form genuine connections.

When she returned with the drinks, she found Mandy and Alfred admiring a painting on her wall. Olivia stood slightly apart, her arms crossed as if hugging herself.

"I was just telling Alfred," Mandy said, accepting her glass, "that this painting reminds me of the one we saw at the craft fair at the fire station last summer. Remember, honey?"

Alfred nodded, a fond smile on his bearded face. "Sure do. You kept saying how nice it'd look in our living room, but we couldn't quite swing it with the budget that month."

Sam handed Alfred and Olivia their glasses. "It does have that homey feel, doesn't it? I actually found this one at a yard sale down the street. Can you believe someone was giving it away?"

"A yard sale? Well, aren't you the savvy shopper, Sam?" Mandy exclaimed, clearly impressed. "I swear, I could spend all day at those sales and never spot a gem like this. You've obviously got a knack for finding hidden treasures."

Olivia, who had been quiet until now, spoke up. "It's lovely, Sam. You have a great eye for these things." Her voice was soft, and Sam saw how tired she looked.

"Thank you, Olivia," Sam said gently. "How about we all sit down? I'd love to hear what everyone's been up to lately."

As they settled into their seats, Sam noticed how Olivia chose the chair closest to the door, as if anticipating a quick escape if needed. She made a mental note to keep an eye on her friend throughout the evening.

She was about to sit down when the doorbell rang again.

"That'll be Derek and Vanessa," she said, setting her own glass down. "Make yourselves at home. I'll be right back."

A minute later, Sam returned with the couple in tow. Derek and Vanessa Martin, who were new to the neighborhood, were at the front door, bore another bottle of wine and gave smiles to the group. Sam introduced them to the rest of the guests.

"Oh, I already know them both," said Dom with a smirk.

Derek gave him a stiff smile.

"We have quite the group assembled here tonight, Sam. What an interesting guest list you've lumped together. Alfred, my man," Dom drawled, swirling his freshly poured whiskey, "I see you're still shopping at the same secondhand stores. How quaint."

Alfred's cheeks reddened, but before he could respond, Mandy jumped in. "Not everyone needs overpriced labels to feel good about themselves."

Dom's eyebrows shot up. "Oh? And I suppose your own 'vintage' look is a conscious choice then?"

Olivia touched her husband's arm. "Dom, please—"

This dinner party was already shaping up to be a disaster, and they hadn't even sat down to eat yet. Everyone looked on edge. Then Sam saw Dom smirking and gripped her hands into fists before forcing herself to relax. Clearly, it was time to switch things up. The problem was Dom. She couldn't take the rest of the guest list into the kitchen to escape him. She'd focus on him.

"Dom, can you give me a hand in the kitchen?"

Sam could tell that, for a few split seconds, Dom thought about treating the question as a genuine question instead of a rhetorical one. That would have been an error, as Sam's face clearly indicated to him. He gave a slight shrug of his shoulders and followed Sam into the kitchen.

Sam wasn't really one to beat around the bush. "What's going on, Dom? Having a rough day?" She took the herb-crusted roast beef out of the oven.

"No." He took a long sip out of the crystal highball glass he was holding. "What did you need my help with?"

She said, "I need your help making this evening go better than it started."

Dom raised his eyebrows. "Am I getting a lecture?"

"If the tables were turned, wouldn't you be lecturing me?"

Dom snorted.

"I'm sorry you've had a bad day, but you either need to fix it moving forward, or say you have a headache and bow out tonight. There's no point in making everybody else have a bad day just because you did."

Dom gave her a cool look. "Isn't there?"

Sam shrugged. "If that's the way you feel, there's no point staying. I can drive you home."

Now Dom's expression was positively frigid. "I don't need anyone's help driving."

Which only served to make Sam determined to find and hide his keys. He strode angrily out of the kitchen while Sam stayed behind to get everything from the oven on the table. She would need to rush things along if the night was going to be a disaster. There was no point lingering over dinner if Dom was set on making everyone miserable.

Before heading out with the food, Sam made her way to her office where the coats, scarves, and gloves were. She'd remembered Dom's full-length black wool coat from when he'd come in. She reached into the pockets and found the keys. She removed them, hiding them in her desk drawer. Then she headed back to the kitchen to bring the food to the dining room and call her guests for supper.

Everyone gathered around the table. Sam was pleased to see Dom was quiet, at least for the time being. Maybe he was the kind of person who went through different stages of drinking. She could use a stage that wasn't belligerent. Even better if he simply dozed off at the table. She could send him home with food later.

Then Dom roused again, much to Sam's disappointment. She saw a cruel look in his eyes as he listened to the other guests chat. She had the feeling he was about to say something unkind, and Sam wasn't sure she was going to keep from snapping at him if he did. Arlo, next to Sam under the table, had his ears back as if he were as uncomfortable as she was by the tone in the room.

Mandy, bless her, was trying to make the mood a little lighter. To bring everything back to a sense of civility. "Derek and Vanessa, are you new to Sunset Ridge? Or just the neighborhood? How are you liking it here?"

Derek smiled at her, looking relieved to have the conversation back on familiar small-talk territory. "Actually, we've been in town for years. But we're new to the neighborhood, to Maple Hills."

"We're enjoying it so far," said Vanessa quickly.

"Have you met many people?" asked Sam. Being the HOA president, she'd gone over with food and a neighborhood directory soon after they'd moved in. But she hadn't stayed long since she didn't want to hold up their unpacking.

"Actually, a good friend of mine lives here, so we came in already knowing someone," said Derek. "He's Aiden Wood. We teach at the same school."

Sam was glad she could keep herself from coloring this time. Even when she'd started dating her ex-husband, she hadn't been this bad about blushing. She wasn't sure what was wrong with her. She and Aiden had probably only shared a conversation six or seven times.

Sam was quickly distracted from thoughts of Aiden when she heard Dom taking on Jason, Olivia's younger brother. From what Sam had seen of Jason, he didn't have a lot of self-confidence. He'd been going through a rough patch where he was between jobs and needed a place to stay. Jason had moved in with Olivia and Dom, likely as temporarily as he could make it, and was using their house as a base while he tried to find work.

Dom was acting as if he and Jason were having a private conversation. Or private argument. "The main problem is that you don't even provide for *yourself*. You're not even bringing in money to pay for your own groceries. You should find a job."

Jason was bright red and looking down at his plate. "That's what I've been trying to do."

"No, I mean a job you're actually qualified to do. Like yard work. Or maybe being a bag boy at the grocery store. That would at least make for a contribution."

Jason's voice was low. "But I have a business degree. I'm qualified to do office work. And finding a job is a full-time job in itself."

"Look, let's get real. You're never going to find a job like that. You're not going to be a success in the business world. You were a mediocre student. We took you in out of pity, but it's time for you to grab the bull by the horns and start working."

Olivia, Jason's sister, was sitting stiffly next to them at the table, pushing her food around with her fork. She finally said in a tremulous voice, "Dom, you were going to check and see if there was something available at the bank."

Dom snorted. "You think I'm going to put my reputation on the line to hire this guy? No thanks. It would be total nepotism, not like I was getting him hired on his merits. He's got to prove his worth first, and he hasn't."

Everyone else at the table had been talking during part of their conversation, but a sudden lull meant everybody was suddenly part of what should have been behind closed doors.

Alfred, always the voice of reason, said quietly, "Hey, maybe this is something you two should talk about later."

Dom turned on him with glittering eyes. "You're defending Jason? I guess since the two of you are pretty much in the same financial situation, that makes sense."

Mandy gave a sharp gasp as if she'd been hit in the stomach. Alfred was clearly trying to take the high road. "Look, let's change the subject and move on. Sam has put together a great dinner, and we need to all work to make it an equally great night."

"*Is* it a great dinner?" asked Dom nastily.

Sam cocked an eyebrow. "If you don't like the food, I have alternatives in the kitchen."

"The food is wonderful," said Olivia hastily. She was flushed and looked both furious and humiliated at the same time.

Dom gave a short laugh. "Well, I guess everything is relative. It's better than the slop you put together for meals."

Sam stood up from the table. "Dom, maybe you'd be more comfortable back at home. I'll drive you there."

His eyes narrowed to slits. "I told you I don't need any rides."

"Then you can walk back. It isn't far. And the breeze is bracing enough to help clear your head." Sam was very glad she'd hidden Dom's keys away. She didn't like the determined look in his eyes.

Suddenly, there was a knock at the door. Everyone looked at Sam. She smiled brightly. "Well, all my guests are present and accounted for, so I'm not sure who this is." She stood and walked briskly to the door.

When she opened the door, she was dismayed to see Nora there, her wizened face set in its usual expression of dissatisfaction. Worse than that, Nora was standing with another woman as if she'd taken upon herself not only to crash Sam's dinner party, but to bring someone else along for the ride.

Chapter Two

"Well, hello there!" Nora chirped, her features now taking on a mock pleasant expression. "Rachel and I thought we'd join your little dinner party."

Sam's mind raced. She'd deliberately not invited Nora, worried about how she might interact with the others. And now here she was, with Rachel in tow. Rachel, an attractive woman in her thirties with a broad face and curly hair, stood slightly behind Nora, somehow looking both eager and apologetic. Sam forced a smile. "What a surprise. We're actually in the middle of dinner."

"Perfect timing, then," said Nora, pushing past Sam into the foyer. "I'm starving."

Rachel gave Sam an apologetic look. "I'm so sorry. Nora insisted."

Sam gave a tight smile. "It's fine. Come on in."

As they entered the dining room, all conversation stopped. Dom's eyes narrowed as he caught sight of Rachel. "Well, if it isn't the failed restaurateur," he drawled. "Come to beg for a loan?"

Rachel's face flushed. "I wouldn't take your money if you begged me, Dom."

Olivia looked between them, confusion clear on her face. "Dom, what's the issue between you two?"

Before he could answer, Nora piped up. "Oh, everyone knows about Dom's little vendetta against Rachel's restaurant. It was the talk of the town."

Sam felt a headache coming on.

"Ladies," Sam said, trying to regain control, "while it's lovely to see you both, I'm afraid we don't have enough place settings for extras."

Nora waved a dismissive hand. "Oh, pish posh. We can make room. Scoot over, Alfred, there's a dear."

As Nora grabbed a chair from the corner and wedged herself between a startled Alfred and Mandy, Sam tried to come up with a plan. She could feel her carefully orchestrated dinner party slipping through her fingers.

"So, Rachel," Vanessa said, clearly trying to diffuse the tension, "what have you been up to lately?"

Rachel's smile was tight. "Oh, this and that. Trying to rebuild my life after certain people decided to destroy it." Her gaze flickered meaningfully to Dom.

Dom leaned back in his chair, a smug grin on his face. "Now, now. Don't blame me for your own incompetence."

"That's enough," Sam cut in, her voice sharper than she intended. "Let's enjoy our meal, shall we?" She took a deep breath. She was rapidly losing control of the situation. And Sam was so very fond of being in control.

As she hurried back to the kitchen to fetch extra plates, Sam could hear Nora's voice carrying through the house. "Such drama! This is much more exciting than my evening plans of watching TV with Precious." Precious was Nora's pit bull and apparently quite the TV viewer.

Sam closed her eyes and took a deep breath. It was going to be a long night. Arlo, sensing her distress, padded over and rested his head on her knee. At least someone was on her side.

Sam gritted her teeth into a smile. She'd hosted guests many times over the years, but this was by far the worst dinner party she'd ever thrown. She stepped back into the dining room with the plates.

Dom stood up abruptly from the table. He muttered something about having a smoke, then headed out toward the terrace.

Sam glanced around the table. Mandy and Alfred both looked indignant and uncomfortable. Olivia and Jason looked as if they wanted to sink into the floor. Derek seemed awkward, as if he wasn't exactly sure what to say or do. His wife, Vanessa, was looking after Dom with a strange expression on her face. Rachel seemed torn between indignation at Dom and gate-crashing guilt. Nora was simply looking smug.

Everyone was quiet for a few moments. Then Olivia took a deep breath. "I can't apologize enough, everyone. I hope you don't think too poorly of us."

Jason said in a scoffing voice, "What do you mean *us*? It's just Dom. You and I are perfectly well-behaved. And his actions don't reflect on us at all."

"You're right," said Sam after pausing to choose her words carefully. "No one thinks any less of you. As for Dom, we all know everyone has bad days."

"Well, Dom's had a lot of them lately," said Jason darkly.

"Are the two of you okay?" asked Mandy, looking anxious. "I mean, Dom is a handful tonight. Has he been okay to live with?"

Olivia said, "He's not usually this bad. I'm not sure what's on his mind tonight. There must be something really troubling him, from the way he's acting."

"And the way he's drinking," added Jason. He looked as if he was still stung by the things Dom was saying to him earlier. But Jason was drinking quite a bit himself, from what Sam had noted. It was just that his behavior hadn't reflected the alcohol intake.

Nora was pouring herself a large glass of wine, as if the mention of drinking reminded her she could do with a little something. "I say we put Dom out of our heads. Let him go enjoy his cigarette and maybe he'll come back better-behaved. Now it's time for the rest of us to have a good time. Especially after all the effort Sam has gone to in order to make everything perfect."

Sam appreciated Nora's attempt to lighten the mood, even as she inwardly cringed at the thought of Dom alone on her terrace. She could only hope he wouldn't accidentally set fire to her carefully cultivated potted plants.

"You're right, Nora," Sam said, forcing a smile. "Let's try to salvage this evening. Who's ready for dessert?"

Rachel, still looking uncomfortable, leaned over to Sam. "I'm so sorry for crashing your party," she whispered. "I can leave if you want. I feel terrible about all this."

Sam shook her head. "No, no. You're here now. Might as well stay for dessert." She paused, then added with a wry smile, "Besides, I made enough meringues to feed a small army. I could use the help eating them."

As Sam bustled about serving dessert, she couldn't help but notice the strange dynamics playing out around her table. Jason was glowering into his wineglass, while Olivia kept casting worried glances toward the terrace. Alfred and Mandy were giving each other worried looks over Nora's head. Derek and Vanessa looked increasingly uncomfortable. And Nora . . . well, Nora was on her second generous glass of wine and looking like she was settling in for a show.

Everyone seemed restless. Enough that they either ate dessert quickly or didn't at all. Instead, they all rose from the table as soon as possible, milling around the living room, dining room, and kitchen, engaging in conversation or looking uncomfortable or both.

Olivia wasn't the only one worried about Dom on the terrace. Sam decided she should check on Dom. After all, Jason had reported earlier that the wind was overpowering out there. Dom had been out there a long time. Had he fallen asleep? Was he getting frostbitten? He hadn't gone into the office to even get his coat.

As she headed toward the terrace to assess the situation, Arlo at her heels, she couldn't shake the terrible feeling that this was the beginning of a very long, very complicated evening.

"Come on, boy," she murmured to Arlo. "Let's go see what fresh hell awaits us out there."

She picked up the little dog, thinking his thin coat wouldn't be enough to keep him warm on the windy terrace in November. But when she walked outside, she didn't see Dom. Although, when the wind gusted, she smelled cigarette smoke.

"Where did he go?" she asked Arlo. "Did he walk back home?" Sam experienced a great deal of relief at the thought.

Arlo wriggled in her arms, which was most unlike Arlo. He was usually happy to be held.

"What's wrong? Do you need to use the bathroom?" Although that didn't seem quite right. She'd let Arlo out shortly before everyone had arrived, and he never had to go out very often.

She carefully set the little dog down.

Arlo trotted over to the edge of the terrace, looking down the stone stairs that led to the acres of land below. He turned to look around at her with beseeching eyes.

Sam had a bad feeling in the pit of her stomach. "What is it, Arlo?" She walked over to join him.

And there she saw Dom Stanton, sprawled at the bottom of the stone staircase.

Chapter Three

S am felt her heart leap into her throat. For a moment, she stood frozen, her mind refusing to process what she was seeing. Then instinct kicked in.

"Dom?" she called out, her voice shaky. "Dom, can you hear me?"

There was no response. The only sound was the whistle of the wind and Arlo's low whine.

"Arlo, wait," said Sam. Arlo immediately sat down, staying perfectly still. Sam quickly descended the stairs, her legs trembling beneath her. As she reached Dom's motionless form, she knew instantly that something was terribly wrong. Sam saw in the bright light of the full moon that his body was twisted at an unnatural angle, his eyes staring blankly at the night sky.

With shaking hands, she felt for a pulse.

"No," Sam whispered. She took a deep breath, forcing herself to think clearly. She needed to call for help.

She walked inside through the kitchen door, Arlo at her heels. Her phone was on its charger on the counter. She gave the 911 operator her location and name, and reported a fall. At least, she hoped it was a fall.

When she re-entered the dining room, all eyes turned to her. The laughter and chatter died instantly as they took in her pale face and wide eyes.

"Sam?" Olivia asked, her voice laced with concern. "What's wrong? Where's Dom?"

Sam swallowed hard. "There's been an accident," she said, her voice barely above a whisper. "Dom fell down the stairs. I'm afraid he didn't make it, Olivia. I'm so sorry."

The room erupted into chaos. Olivia let out a strangled cry while Jason jumped to his feet to comfort his sister, nearly knocking over his chair in the process. Nora gasped dramatically, her hand flying to her mouth.

The next hour passed in a blur. Police cars and an ambulance arrived, their lights painting the quiet neighborhood in flashes of red and blue. Lieutenant Warren Phillips, a tall man in early middle age with cropped dark hair, took charge of the scene.

As the guests were questioned one by one, Sam found herself sitting on her couch, Arlo curled up beside her. She heard her name being called and looked up in surprise. Aiden Wood was standing there, a concerned look on his features.

"Aiden," she said, looking confused. "What are you doing here?" Then she remembered. "Once a police officer, always a police officer, right?"

He gave her a small smile. "Sorry, I didn't mean to gatecrash. I wanted to see if I could help out when I saw all the emergency vehicles outside. And, yeah, I know the guys who are here from when I was on the force. I talked to one of them on the way in, and he filled me in on what happened." He paused, flushing a little. "I was worried about you."

"Thanks. It's been quite a night. I'm glad you came. Besides, you weren't the only one to show up uninvited," said Sam wryly in a low voice. "Nora and Rachel were unexpected guests, too." Sam cleared her throat, feeling as if she ought to apologize for not inviting Aiden. "Hey, I didn't mean to exclude you from an invite. I was trying to do something really small, for my first foray back into the social scene." She didn't mention that she'd rather see Aiden on a more one-on-one basis, maybe for a date, at some point in the future. Although she wasn't totally sure she was quite up to it yet. But she was getting there.

Aiden was already shaking his head. "That's the last thing on my mind. You've been through the wringer lately, Sam, with everything that happened with Chad. And, really, you're still adjusting to a new home and town, even though you've gotten very involved here."

Sam nodded, grateful for his calm presence amidst the chaos. As Detective Phillips approached them, Sam straightened her spine, preparing herself for what was to come.

"Ms. Prescott," the detective said, his voice grave. "I'm afraid I have some difficult news. Based on our preliminary investigation, we don't believe Mr. Stanton's death was accidental."

"You're saying this was murder?"

"We're treating this as a potential homicide. And I'm going to need you and your guests to answer some tough questions."

Chapter Four

S am watched as Detective Phillips conferred with the local
police chief, a stocky man named Bill Hawkins, who had arrived shortly after the state police. The small-town police force
was clearly out of its depth with a potential homicide, and Sam
was relieved to see the more experienced state investigator taking charge.

"Folks," Chief Hawkins addressed the room, his voice gruff
but not unkind, "we're going to need to speak with each of you
individually. Detective Phillips here will be conducting the interviews in Ms. Prescott's home office. In the meantime, I'm
afraid you'll all need to stay put until we've finished our preliminary investigation."

Phillips nodded, his expression grave. "We appreciate your
cooperation. This is a difficult situation for everyone, but it's
crucial that we gather all the information we can while events
are still fresh in your minds."

As the detective and the chief stepped away to set up in the
office, Sam found herself at a loss. Her guests, now potential suspects, sat in tense silence, avoiding each other's eyes. Arlo, sens-

ing the unease in the room, paced between the guests, his tail low and eyes worried.

"Are you okay?" Sam quietly asked Olivia. Olivia, tight-lipped, nodded.

"Would anyone like more dessert?" Sam offered weakly, desperate to do something, anything, to break the oppressive atmosphere. "Or maybe some coffee? I think we could all use something warm."

Nora, surprisingly, was the first to respond. "I wouldn't say no to a cup. And perhaps a splash of brandy in it, if you have any. For medicinal purposes."

Sam nodded, glad to have a task. As she busied herself in the kitchen, she could hear the murmur of low voices from the living room. Arlo followed her, his paws clicking softly on the tile floor.

"What do you make of all this, Arlo?" she whispered to the dog as she set up the coffeemaker. Arlo tilted his head, his eyes never leaving her face. "Yeah, I don't know either."

As she waited for the coffee to brew, Sam thought back to what she'd seen on the terrace. No matter how difficult Dom had been, he certainly didn't deserve what had happened to him. And if it was murder, it was clear one of her guests was the perpetrator.

The coffeemaker beeped, jolting Sam back to the present. She poured the steaming liquid into mugs. As she added a generous splash of brandy to Nora's cup, she heard Detective Phillips call out from the office.

"Ms. Prescott? We'd like to start with you, if you don't mind."

Sam took a deep breath, steeling herself. She gave Arlo a final pat on the head before heading toward the office, leaving the dog to watch over her shell-shocked guests.

As she entered the room, Phillips gestured for her to take a seat. "Ms. Prescott," he began, his voice professional but not unkind, "I know this is difficult, but I need you to walk me through everything that happened this evening, from the moment your guests arrived until you found Mr. Stanton. Don't leave anything out, no matter how insignificant it might seem."

"Okay," said Sam, thinking it all through. In her mind, the evening had morphed into a blurry mess. And the fact of the matter was, she'd discovered his body. Sam supposed she'd have to be eliminated as a suspect herself. "First off, Dom was in a rotten mood as soon as he came in."

"Quiet? Sullen?"

Sam shook her head. "Not quiet, unfortunately. Belligerent. Snide."

Phillips studied her. "Did Dom say why he was in such a bad mood? Had something happened at work? At home?"

"He didn't say. He definitely wasn't making excuses or apologizing for his behavior."

Phillips nodded. "Can you tell me who he was directing his ire at?"

Sam gave a short laugh. "Just about everybody. He even told me the food wasn't any good." She paused again. "Of course, that's hardly motive for murder, although it did irritate me."

"How well do you know the Stantons?"

Sam said, "I don't know Dom well, but he's always been polite when I've seen him. I know Olivia much better. We've become friends and volunteer together."

"Has Olivia mentioned having trouble in her marriage?"

Sam took a deep breath. She didn't think Olivia had murdered her husband, but she was sure the detective considered her a suspect. Wasn't it usually the spouse in these types of situations? She carefully answered. "No, she hasn't said anything directly. But I know she was always very careful around Dom. Olivia didn't want to make him upset."

"Was he abusive?" asked Phillips.

Sam paused. "Not that I'm aware."

Phillips jotted down some notes. "Okay. Who was Dom being belligerent toward?"

"Well, there was Jason Barnes. He's Olivia's brother. Jason has been living with them for a while now because he's been out of work. Dom was giving him a hard time." That was a mild way of putting it. Dom was unrelenting in his criticism of Jason.

"A hard time about what?" Phillips raised his eyebrows.

"Just that he was being a financial burden. That he wasn't contributing to household costs. And that he wasn't qualified to do more than low-paying jobs."

"Is that all true?" asked Phillips.

"I don't really know. He seems bright and motivated to me. There probably aren't a lot of opportunities out there right now."

Phillips jotted down another couple of notes. Then he looked back at Sam. "Can you tell me why you invited Dom and Jason to your dinner party? I'd have thought maybe just inviting your friend Olivia would have been enough."

Sam took a moment to collect her thoughts before continuing. "Olivia's become a good friend since I moved here, and I wanted to include her family. I thought it might be nice for them to have an evening out together."

She paused, then added, "The purpose of tonight was really to put myself back out there in the neighborhood again. As you know, I'm new here, and after everything that happened with my ex-husband . . ." She trailed off, then shook her head. "I wanted a fresh start. To show everyone that I'm not defined by what happened with Chad. I thought hosting a fairly small dinner party would be a good way to connect with my neighbors and start building a new life here."

Phillips nodded, scribbling more notes. "I see. And what about Dom's interactions with the other guests? You mentioned he was belligerent toward Jason. What about the others?"

Sam frowned, recalling the events of the evening. "Well, he was pretty unpleasant to Alfred. He made some snide comments about his clothes, implying they were cheap or secondhand. Alfred and Mandy aren't as well-off as others, and Dom seemed to take pleasure in pointing that out."

"And how did Alfred react?"

"He was clearly upset, but he tried to take the high road. Mandy looked like she wanted to say something, but she held back."

Phillips made another note. "Anyone else?"

"Yes, when he greeted Vanessa and Derek Martin, he was . . . smarmy, I guess you could say. Especially toward Vanessa. It made her visibly uncomfortable."

"Can you elaborate on that?"

Sam shifted in her seat. "It was the way he looked at her, the tone of his voice. It was overly familiar, almost flirtatious, but in a way that felt sort of off. Derek noticed it too. I saw him frowning."

"I see," Phillips said. "And what about when Rachel arrived?"

"She and Nora showed up unexpectedly. When Dom saw Rachel, his whole demeanor changed, and he became even more antagonistic."

"How so?"

"He made a comment about her being a 'failed restaurateur' and asked if she was there to beg him for a loan. It was clear there was bad blood between them."

Phillips leaned forward. "Did you know about any history between Dom and Rachel?"

Sam shook her head. "No, I didn't. But from their interaction, it was obvious there was something there. Rachel looked furious, and Dom liked making her uncomfortable."

Phillips tapped his pen on the paper. "And you have no idea what set Dom off like this?"

"Well, alcohol didn't help, but he was behaving like that right out of the gate. I think he might have had a drink or two before he even came over."

Phillips said, "Can you tell me where you were when Dom was outside? And where everyone else was?"

Sam gave a short laugh. "That's not a straightforward question to answer at a party. We were all at the table to begin with, eating dessert. That course didn't last long since everyone seemed restless and ready to get up and move around. I was trying to be a good hostess, so I was making conversation with different guests, refilling drinks, and taking food in and out of the kitchen."

"No one had eyes on you the entire time."

Sam said, "I really doubt it. There would have been no reason for a guest to be staring at me during the whole party. They were all trying to relax, having drinks, and chatting."

"Even the two gatecrashers?"

"Even Rachel and Nora. I could tell Rachel felt uncomfortable about showing up and making a scene. Nora, on the other hand, was pleased as punch to be there." Sam gave a wry smile.

"And you don't have any idea where people were while Dom was on the terrace? After they all got up from the table?"

Sam considered the question. "Not really. I got the sense Vanessa might have stepped away for a minute or two."

Phillips raised his eyebrows. "Out on the terrace?"

"No, no. Maybe to the bathroom or something. Everyone was drinking, so there were trips to the bathroom happening. No one was gone for long."

Phillips said, "Of course, it wouldn't take long to push someone down a staircase."

"No, I suppose not." Sam felt a frisson of fear go up her spine. Someone had murdered Dom at her house. One of her guests appeared to be a killer.

"It sounds like Rachel really went out of her way to take on Dom. At least, I'm guessing that's the reason she showed up at your dinner party. You said you don't know her?" asked Phillips.

Sam shook her head. "No. We hadn't formally met before tonight. I got the feeling Nora talked Rachel into coming tonight. But once Rachel saw Dom, she was ready to fight with him."

"Fight?"

"Argue, I mean." Sam realized it was probably important to be exact here.

"And you didn't know Dom very well?" Phillips was studying her thoughtfully.

"Only as the spouse of a friend. I didn't have anything against the man, if you're trying to come up with motives. Although I wasn't very pleased by his behavior tonight." Which was decidedly an understatement.

Phillips stood up, and Sam followed suit. "Okay. Thanks for the overview. Could you send Rachel in, please?"

Chapter Five

Sam left the office. She found her guests in the living room, looking restless. Everyone seemed to have stopped eating and drinking. Olivia was sitting on the sofa next to her brother, her eyes red-rimmed from tears or tiredness or both. Sam asked Rachel to join Phillips in the office.

"Is everyone okay?" Sam asked. "Do you need anything?"

She was asking the entire group, but her eyes were focused on Olivia, who was staring blankly at the floor. "Do you want a glass of water?" asked Jason solicitously. Olivia nodded her head dully.

"Water is a good idea," said Sam. She left the room with relief, glad to escape the mood for a minute. She returned a couple of minutes later with a pitcher of water and a stack of plastic cups.

Olivia stood up to head to the bathroom. She came back with her face scrubbed and looking a little more alert than she had before.

"I'm so sorry," Sam said gently to her. There was nothing else really to say.

"I don't know how I'll make it on my own," she said in a trembling voice.

"I know it'll be hard at first, but you'll be able to find your way. You're a lot stronger than you think," said Sam.

Olivia nodded slightly, then headed off to join her brother on the sofa again.

Mandy walked over to Derek to speak with him. Derek's wife, Vanessa, was looking drained and watched as the police secured the terrace with crime scene tape.

Nora was apparently taking it upon herself to tidy up the living and dining rooms. "Oh, don't worry about that," said Sam quickly.

Nora tutted. "What if the police want to inspect the rest of the downstairs? Can't have them thinking we're slovenly, can we?" She kept picking up plates and glasses and moving them into the kitchen. Sam supposed if the police didn't want Nora that close to the terrace, they'd surely let her know.

Arlo watched Nora with curious eyes, following her around the room as if supervising her work. Then he picked up a dropped napkin in his mouth, proudly presenting it to Nora as his contribution to the cleanup effort.

"Aren't you a helpful little man?" said Nora, bending to rub the dog. "Clever, just like my Precious. Much more useful than some of the two-legged creatures around here."

Sam noticed Nora casting furtive glances toward the closed door of Sam's office, where the interviews were taking place. Nora would pause by the door, ostensibly to dust a nearby shelf with the napkin Arlo had provided her.

Nora caught Sam looking at her and flushed. "Just making sure everyone's being treated fairly by the officer," she said with a sniff.

Sam gave her a small smile and walked off to join Mandy, who was standing with the new neighbor, Derek.

Mandy said in a low voice, "I bet the police think we're all suspects. Imagine Dom acting the way he did tonight! The very idea," she said indignantly.

Derek nodded. "He was baiting everybody this evening. No one was really unscathed." He looked at Sam. "Although I don't think he went after you."

"Well, he criticized my cooking," said Sam ruefully. She glanced over at Olivia to make sure she was out of earshot. Like Vanessa, Olivia seemed exhausted and sort of out of it.

Aiden joined the group, his eyes immediately seeking Derek. There was a flash of concern on his face as he approached his friend and fellow teacher. "Hey, man," he said softly, clasping Derek's shoulder. "How are you holding up?"

Derek gave a wan smile, grateful for the familiar presence. "As well as can be expected, I guess. It's all still sinking in."

Aiden nodded, understanding in his eyes. He'd known Derek long enough to read the tension in his shoulders, the slight furrow in his brow that betrayed his discomfort. Turning to the group, Aiden asked, "Everything okay here?"

"Not really," said Mandy sadly. She added, "You used to be a cop, Aiden, right? What are the police thinking right now?"

"If it's a homicide, which it appears they think it is, they're focusing on using correct protocol and making sure they're asking all the right questions."

Sam added, "Like asking where each of us was while Dom was out on the terrace."

"Oh mercy," said Mandy. "Everybody was all over the place at that point. Dom wasn't even cooperative enough tonight to at least go outside when everyone was at the table during the main course. Then it would have been a piece of cake to see who murdered him."

Derek said, "I never left the dining room. I really liked that meringue. Dom must have been hallucinating when he was criticizing the food."

Sam gave him a small smile. "Thanks. Yeah, I was all over the place, like I told Detective Phillips."

"You were just being a great hostess," said Mandy staunchly. "You were making sure your guests had everything they needed." She thought for a moment. "You know, I don't really remember exactly what I was doing. I talked to Olivia for a few minutes. She was *so* embarrassed about the way Dom was acting. I tried to reassure her again that it was totally fine. Everybody has a bad day every now and then. I got another drink, I ate more dessert. I kept looking nervously toward the door to make sure Dom wasn't coming back in and attacking all of us some more."

Derek looked over toward the sofa where Olivia was still looking blankly out at the police officers. "Olivia must be really torn up about this," he mumbled, his voice barely above a whisper, checking to make sure she wasn't overhearing the conversation.

"She's always seemed very devoted to Dom," Aiden remarked, his tone carefully neutral. As the longest-standing resident in their group, Aiden had likely observed the Stantons' relationship over the years, but he kept his thoughts to himself.

Mandy, ever the nurturer, leaned forward. "The poor thing. I'll bring some food by for her tomorrow. Maybe a nice chicken casserole."

Derek nodded absently, his gaze drifting over to his wife. Sam couldn't help but notice that Vanessa seemed almost as upset as Olivia, her face pale and her hands trembling slightly. But then again, it had been an incredibly upsetting evening. A sudden death at a dinner party would shake anyone to their core.

Mandy, still visibly rattled by Dom's behavior throughout the evening, hesitated before speaking again. "I understand Olivia being devastated by losing her husband like that. It's awful. But, well, do you think she had a happy marriage?"

The question hung in the air, heavy with implication. It was the same question Sam had been mulling over. Olivia did seem close to Dom, despite her brief affair months ago. But she'd been terrified of Dom finding out about it. Was that simply guilt, or was there something more sinister at play?

Before anyone could answer, Mandy pressed on. "I thought Dom was rather unkind to you too, Derek. At least, his tone was unpleasant. Did you know him very well? I know you're new to the neighborhood."

Derek shifted uncomfortably in his seat. "New to the neighborhood, but not new to Sunset Ridge," he reminded them. "I do know Dom, although not well. He was never my favorite person, but there was no real tension between us." He paused, seeming to weigh his next words carefully. "I'd heard he might be cheating on his wife."

Mandy's eyes grew wide, and Aiden leaned forward. "That's a rumor going around?" Aiden asked, his tone casual but his eyes sharp.

"Yes, it's a rumor," Derek said, his voice low. "But I've heard it from a couple of different people. Reliable sources, if you can call gossip reliable."

Sam, sensing an opportunity, jumped in. "Have you heard anything about Dom's relationship with alcohol? Has it been changing? Getting worse?"

Derek ran a hand through his hair, looking increasingly uncomfortable. "I'm afraid I don't know much about that. But judging from what I saw tonight, it couldn't have been a healthy relationship. He seemed different."

"Different how?" Sam pressed gently.

Derek sighed. "Dom was always a bit of a strong personality. But tonight, he seemed almost unhinged. The way he spoke to Jason, to Alfred, even the looks he was giving my wife. It was like he didn't care about consequences anymore."

"And how did that make you feel?" Aiden asked, his tone still casual but his eyes never leaving Derek's face.

Derek's jaw tightened. "Honestly? It made me angry. Dom had no right to treat people that way, especially in someone else's home. But I never . . ." He trailed off, shaking his head. "I never would have wished this on him."

The room fell silent for a moment, thinking about Dom's fate out on the terrace.

"Is there anything else you can tell us about Dom?" Sam asked. "Anything that might help us understand what happened tonight?"

Derek hesitated, then shook his head. "Nothing specific. But I got the feeling that Dom was a guy with a lot of secrets. And in a small town like this, secrets eventually have a way of coming out."

The evening seemed to drag on with Detective Phillips calling each one of the guests in individually for statements.

After her turn with Phillips, Rachel came over to Sam, an apologetic look once again on her face. "I'm so sorry again about tonight."

Sam said graciously, "Don't worry about it anymore. You've already apologized. It's water under the bridge."

"I'd feel a lot better if I had the opportunity to make it up to you, though. Since the restaurant failed, I've been giving cooking classes for a little income. I'd love to give you a free one." She quickly added, "I know you're a great cook. Everything you served tonight was fabulous."

"A cooking class would be great," said Sam brightly. It would also offer her the opportunity to find out more about Rachel, of course. And her issues with Dom.

As it happened, Rachel had an opening the next day, at her home, at two in the afternoon. They called it a plan.

After a short while longer, everyone was free to leave. Sam dug Dom's keys out of her desk and gave them to Olivia. She gave solemn goodbyes to her guests as they filed out.

"Can you find alternate accommodations for the night?" Phillips asked her. "The crime scene investigators are on their way and will need to thoroughly examine the scene. Perhaps with a friend?"

Considering how completely exhausted she felt, Sam didn't feel much like being someone's houseguest for the night, nor putting anyone out. She felt more like being alone, unwinding, mulling over what had happened, and then having a very solid night's sleep. "I'll stay in a hotel overnight."

Aiden, who was still there, said, "With Arlo?"

"Of course with Arlo. I'm sure there must be at least one hotel in town that will take us both."

Arlo grinned winningly at Sam and Aiden as if to show what a truly exemplary animal he was.

"I'll make a few phone calls for you," offered Aiden, stepping away.

Phillips looked thoughtfully after Aiden. "It was nice that he came over to help tonight."

Sam felt her blush rising again and silently cursed it. "Yes, it was." She cleared her throat. "Is it possible for me to put together an overnight bag? To run upstairs?"

"Of course."

Chapter Six

$\mathcal{S}$ am left to gather a few things from her bedroom and bathroom before heading back downstairs again to join Aiden and Phillips, who were talking with each other.

Aiden said, "Good news. The Ridgeview House downtown has vacancies and will take both you and Arlo."

"Great," said Sam. She grabbed a few things for Arlo while she was downstairs, putting them in a tote bag she pulled from the coat closet.

Phillips studied her a moment. "Are you sure you're all right to drive? It's been an upsetting evening."

Upsetting was an understatement. "I'm sure I'll be fine," said Sam. "I feel totally exhausted, but still very keyed up." It was almost as if she might be too tired to fall asleep.

Aiden seemed to hesitate for a moment. Then he said, "How about if I join you over at the hotel's bar for a drink? That might help you unwind a little before you turn in. And it wouldn't hurt me, either."

Sam gave him a smile. "Perfect. I have the feeling you haven't had a drop of all this alcohol, and I only had a bit of wine that I bolted when Dom was bullying everyone earlier."

They took separate cars over to The Ridgeview. It was perched on a gentle slope overlooking downtown Sunset Ridge. The hotel was a lovingly restored Greek Revival home, dating back to the 1870s. The two-story, pale blue clapboard building was accented with white columns and black shutters, giving it a stately but welcoming appearance. A spacious veranda wrapped around the front and side of the house, furnished with cushioned wicker chairs.

After Sam and Arlo checked in, they headed to a cozy parlor off the main foyer where Aiden was already waiting. The room was dominated by an original brick fireplace and a sturdy wooden mantel. A pair of comfortable armchairs flanked the hearth, each accompanied by a small side table. "There's an honor bar," he said with a grin. "There are a few wines and some local craft beers to choose from. You list your name and what you selected in that ledger there."

"Perfect," said Sam, taking Arlo off his leash. "What do you want?"

"Oh, I can leave a few dollars at the front desk."

"Nope. None of that. You were very helpful tonight, despite not being on the original guest list." Sam gave him an apologetic look. "The very least I can do is buy you a drink or two."

"Just one, and thanks."

Sam opened the lean, stainless-steel refrigerator and pulled out two local IPAs.

Aiden quirked a brow. "You're a beer drinker?"

"Of course. I like beer and wine. Beer has the added benefit of making me feel sleepy. Which, I believe, is the end goal here."

They opened their beers and poured them into two glasses. The room was a fairly relaxing one to sit in, and Sam felt the tension drain from her shoulders. Whether that was because of the atmosphere or Aiden, she couldn't be sure. But then, this was a room that really invited relaxation, aside from the alcohol offerings. One wall was lined with floor-to-ceiling bookcases filled with a mix of classics, local authors, and books about the area's history and natural beauty. The hardwood floors were partially covered by a large antique Persian rug.

Sam felt herself melt into the leather armchair. She sighed. Arlo put his little feet up on the side of the chair, and she lifted him carefully into her lap.

Aiden seemed to wait for her to say something to start off the conversation. She guessed this was because he wasn't sure if she wanted to delve into the topic of murder or whether she'd rather focus on lighter areas of conversation.

"How are you holding up?" he asked softly, his eyes filled with concern.

Sam managed a weak smile. "As well as can be expected, I suppose. It's not every day your dinner party ends in a murder investigation."

Aiden nodded, a small smile tugging at the corners of his mouth. "You do know how to throw an unforgettable gathering, I'll give you that."

Despite everything, Sam found herself chuckling. "Not quite what I had in mind when I was planning the menu."

Their eyes met, and for a moment, the tension in the room seemed to dissipate. There was something there, an undercurrent of warmth and understanding that Sam couldn't quite ignore. Aiden's steady gaze held a promise of support, of something more if she wanted it.

But the timing wasn't right. With Chad in prison and the divorce finalized at long last, Sam wasn't ready to explore whatever this was between them. Not yet.

As if sensing her thoughts, Aiden leaned back in his chair, giving her space. "You know I'm here if you need anything, right? Even if it's just to talk."

Sam nodded, grateful for his understanding. "I know. Thank you, Aiden. That means a lot."

Then she decided it might be better to discuss the murder, after all. That way, she wouldn't be tossing and turning with all the details running through her mind all night. "You missed a crazy dinner party," she finally said wryly.

The corners of Aiden's eyes creased. "That's what I understand. Dom was in top form?"

"He was. If top form is acting like a drunken lout and getting oneself murdered." Sam paused. "I should have invited you over."

"Again, that's not something you need to worry about," said Aiden briskly.

"I know, you kindly let me off the hook." They sat in comfortable silence for a few moments before Sam's mind inevitably drifted back to the events of the evening. She began to recap the dinner party, trying to make sense of what had transpired.

"It's strange," she mused aloud. "Looking back, it feels like everyone had some sort of odd tension with Dom."

Aiden raised an eyebrow, encouraging her to continue.

"There was Jason, of course. Dom was totally relentless in his criticism of him. It was more than simply disapproval of Jason's unemployment; it felt personal, like he enjoyed tearing him down."

She paused, remembering the hurt and anger in Jason's eyes. "I felt really sorry for poor Alfred and Mandy. Dom's comments about their finances were so unnecessary. I didn't realize how cruel he could be. I hope Olivia didn't see that side of him often."

"Mandy and Alfred are such great people. I hate that he made them feel so awkward."

"I know," said Sam. "I saw how it affected them, especially Alfred. He was trying so hard to keep his composure."

"What about the Martins?" Aiden asked.

Sam frowned, recalling the odd dynamics she'd observed. "Derek seemed uncomfortable around Dom, but it was more than that. The way Dom looked at Vanessa was unsettling. Like he knew something about her, or about them. And Vanessa looked nervous every time Dom spoke to her."

She shook her head, trying to make sense of it all. "Then there was Rachel. I had no idea there was history there, but Dom's reaction when she arrived was visceral. It was like he couldn't help himself, he had to lash out at her."

"And Olivia?" Aiden prompted gently.

Sam sighed. "Olivia seemed sort of resigned. Like she was used to Dom's behavior and was just trying to keep the peace. But there were moments when I saw something in her eyes. Frustration or maybe anger? I'm not sure."

She shook her head. "It's like Dom had this gift for pushing everyone's buttons, for finding their weak spots and exploiting them. But why? What was he getting out of it?"

Aiden leaned forward, looking thoughtful. "Sometimes people lash out when they're feeling cornered or threatened. I wonder if Dom felt like he was losing control of something in his life, and this was his way of trying to regain it."

Sam nodded slowly, considering this. "Maybe. But what made him feel that way? And did it push someone to the point where they felt murder was the only option of dealing with him?"

They talked for a few more minutes, enjoying the last embers of the fire and the last sips of their beers. Then Aiden said, "I'd better head out. You should get some rest." He reached over and rubbed Arlo, who yawned and gave him a canine grin. They marked down what they'd drunk in the hotel's book.

Sam and Arlo headed to their room. Fifteen minutes later, they were both snoring.

Chapter Seven

The next morning, Sam left Arlo snoozing in the room and headed out for breakfast. She was expecting something continental and was delighted to see fluffy buttermilk biscuits, cheesy scrambled eggs, golden hash browns, and buttery grits. Another small buffet had mini quiches, cinnamon rolls, and blueberry muffins. She splurged and had a little of everything.

However, she found herself completely stuffed. Enough that she wondered if she'd even be up for sampling the results of her cooking class with Rachel at two o'clock.

Sam lingered over her coffee for a few minutes. Maybe it was the harrowing event of the night before that reminded her of Chad. The familiar pang of betrayal twisted in her gut, a feeling she'd grown accustomed to, but still couldn't shake.

"Stop it," she muttered to herself, setting her coffee cup down with more force than necessary. She'd been over this a thousand times in her mind, dissecting every moment of their marriage, searching for signs she might have missed. But the truth was, Chad had hidden his true nature well.

Sam walked back to her room, packed up her belongings, checked out, then set off for home with Arlo. Arlo seemed quite perkier than he had when she'd left him in the room for breakfast. She decided to take him to the dog park to let him run some of that energy out. Plus, she admitted she wasn't exactly eager to get back home again after last night.

"Want to try something new, Arlo?" she asked the little dog.

He grinned at her, apparently up for anything. That was good, because she hadn't yet visited the dog park with Arlo. She'd heard good things about the park itself, but some fair-to-middling things about other dog owners, some of whom apparently didn't do a wonderful job monitoring their pets. But Arlo was so spritely that she decided to give it a go.

She pulled into a parking spot, and she and Arlo headed up to the gated entrance. It was a chilly morning, but the wind wasn't gusting like it was last night. Plus, the sun was out and lent some warmth to the park. Sam read the signs carefully, noting that there were separate sections for large and small dogs. There were open grassy areas and shady spots under mature oaks. Benches and picnic tables dotted the perimeter, and there was a water fountain for both humans and canines.

"What do you think?" she asked Arlo.

Arlo answered with an enthusiastic wag of his tail. With that, Sam and Arlo entered the section for the smaller dogs.

A portly pug was waddling after a tennis ball with more enthusiasm than speed, while a pair of chihuahuas seemed to be engaged in a fierce debate over a stick twice their size.

Arlo, ever the gentleman, politely sniffed a passing Yorkie before deciding the pug's abandoned tennis ball was worth investigating. As he pranced around with his newfound treasure, a sleek whippet zoomed past, startling Arlo into dropping the ball. The whippet, apparently having no interest in the ball, continued its circuit around the park at breakneck speed.

"First time here?" a friendly voice asked. Sam turned to see a woman in her forties with short, spiky hair and an athletic build.

"Is it that obvious?" Sam laughed.

The woman smiled. "I'm Lucy. That blur you see is my whippet, Ziggy."

As they chatted, Lucy's eyes kept darting to Arlo, who was now attempting to join the chihuahuas' stick negotiations.

"Your little guy has great balance and focus," Lucy remarked. "Have you ever thought about agility training?"

Sam raised an eyebrow. "Agility? For Arlo?"

Lucy nodded enthusiastically. "Oh yeah, he'd be perfect. The way he navigates around the other dogs, his attentiveness to you . . . those are great foundations for agility work."

As Arlo returned to Sam's side, Lucy knelt down to his level. "You'd love it, wouldn't you, buddy? Running through tunnels, leaping over jumps. You'd love it."

Arlo's tail wagged furiously at Lucy's tone, causing both women to laugh.

"There's a beginners' class starting next week at the Sunset Ridge Canine Center."

Sam raised her eyebrows. "A canine center. I wouldn't have thought Sunset Ridge was large enough to support something like that."

Lucy grinned at her. "Don't set your expectations too high. One of our members is a real enthusiast and owns a lot of land out here. He set up a modest facility. The club gets together most weeks, aside from classes," Lucy said, standing up. "In fact, we're meeting up tomorrow to practice and hang out. You can find the location online. You should check it out. It's a blast for both dogs and humans."

As Sam watched Arlo confidently trot off to investigate a new arrival, she found herself intrigued by the idea. Maybe agility shows could be a fun new adventure for both of them. One that didn't involve murder.

After a while, Arlo seemed played out. He drank a lot of water from the dog fountain, then they headed back to the car and back home.

The house was in better shape than Sam had expected. Either she hadn't clearly remembered the state it was in when she'd left, or Nora had done more cleaning than Sam realized. She started the dishwasher, wiped down the counters, and took out the trash. Then she took a moment to look outside the window, at the terrace. Steeling herself, she headed out the door, leaving Arlo inside, where he was already curling into his bed to get some sleep.

The crime scene tape had mostly been removed, although they'd left a strand behind. There was a powdery dusting on the terrace railing, apparently from fingerprint dusting. Sam went back inside to get a trash bag and some paper towels and cleaned up for a few minutes. There had been no blood on the steps, she'd noticed, or else the police had cleaned up after forensics was finished with the scene.

Sam came back inside, glad to be out of the cold. She sank onto the sofa, curling her feet under her.

Arlo trotted over, his nails clicking softly on the hardwood floor. He placed his chin on the edge of the sofa, looking up at her with soulful eyes. She scratched behind his ears, smiling as his tail wagged contentedly.

"Want to curl up here before I head to Rachel's cooking class?" Sam asked, glancing at her watch. She still had a little time before she needed to leave.

Arlo's response was to stand up even straighter so Sam could pick him up and place him on the sofa next to her. Arlo circled once before settling down with a contented sigh. She chuckled, running her fingers through his soft fur. They sat in comfortable silence. All too soon, it was time for Sam to head out. She gently lifted Arlo, placing him on his plush bed nearby. "I won't be gone long," she promised, grabbing her keys and coat. "And who knows? Maybe I'll bring back something tasty for you to try."

Chapter Eight

Sam typed Rachel's address into her GPS, glad again that she had the technology to help guide her around Sunset Ridge. She still felt like a new arrival in town, and definitely didn't know any other neighborhoods besides Maple Hills. Her phone guided her to an older neighborhood not too far from downtown.

Rachel's house was a cozy cabin, nestled among tall pines and maples. The exterior was a warm, honey-colored wood with a dark green metal roof that echoed the surrounding forest. A small covered porch stretched across the front, complete with a pair of well-worn rocking chairs and a porch swing that appeared to be put to good use when it wasn't freezing cold outside. A gravel driveway led up to a detached single-car garage.

Rachel opened the door and greeted her before she'd had the chance to ring the doorbell. "Glad you could make it, Sam."

"Me too. I love your house." Sam had stepped into a modest foyer. The space was warm and inviting, with knotty pine walls and slate tile flooring. A rustic coat rack made from repurposed branches stood in one corner, while a small bench with cubbies underneath provided a spot to remove shoes.

The kitchen, visible from the foyer, looked like it was the heart of the home. It wasn't large or fancy, but it seemed well-used and loved. Butcher block countertops showed signs of past meals, and open shelving displayed a mix of everyday dishes and what looked like heirloom china.

They walked toward the kitchen. Sam said, "Wow, that island is great. Is that rock?"

"Thanks!" said Rachel. "It's local river rock. I use the island as prep space and for casual dining, too." Sam saw a couple of mismatched stools tucked underneath.

An overweight gray cat lying in a sunbeam stared with dissatisfaction at Sam from across the room, his eyes narrowed.

"I don't think my visit has been approved by your cat," said Sam wryly.

"Otis? He's very picky about visitors, especially in his kitchen."

"Would he be happier if I went over and petted him?" asked Sam.

"I think he'd be appalled," said Rachel with a laugh. "I wouldn't risk it."

Otis pointedly turned his back to them and looked out the window into the backyard.

"Your Arlo was a friendly guy last night," said Rachel. "A lot friendlier than some of the people."

"He was, wasn't he? He's come a long way."

Rachel asked, "Was he a rescue?"

"In a manner of speaking. I rescued him from a neighbor who had him chained in the front yard all hours of the day and night. Socializing him took less time than I thought it would. Maybe it's because he's innately social."

Rachel nodded, but her mind seemed to be somewhere else as she started pulling ingredients out of the fridge. "Hey, once again, I wanted to tell you how sorry I was about barging in last night." She held up her hand as Sam protested. "I know, I've already apologized a bunch. I really do feel awful about it, though." She sighed. "I've been so focused on Dom Stanton and blaming him for the loss of the restaurant that I haven't been thinking clearly."

Sam said, "I have the feeling Nora might have egged you on."

Rachel snorted. "You could say that. I think she wanted drama in her life."

"That sounds about right. And I'm sure she was peeved I didn't invite her. I couldn't invite everyone in the neighborhood, though, naturally. And Nora has a way of being abrasive sometimes."

"You can say that again," said Rachel.

"How do you know her?" asked Sam. "I mean, everybody in Maple Hills knows her because she lives here and walks Precious every day. But you're not a neighbor."

"She used to be a regular at my restaurant. Actually, she was a regular even when my parents owned it, years and years ago. Nora seemed to take it very personally when I had to shut it down. She called me up right away—I don't even know how she had my phone number. She asked me what happened, and I told her about the negative online reviews and the bad word-of-mouth Dom had given the restaurant."

Sam gave a small smile. "I bet Nora was pretty indignant over that."

"Oh, yeah. She said she had her own reasons for disliking Dom."

Sam remembered Nora felt very sorry for Dom's wife, Olivia, and seemed to have a soft spot for her. "Did she tell you why?"

"Nora said Dom wasn't nice to Olivia, or words to that effect. Anyway, I told her I hadn't had any luck getting in touch with Dom to tell him off about sabotaging my business. She suggested we storm your party."

Sam said, "Well, Nora is the kind of person who makes things happen."

Rachel nodded. Then she glanced at the clock. "Sorry. You had a long night last night and I promised you a cooking class. Here I am yammering about my own issues. So, let's get started, and we can talk more as we work. I've got ingredients prepped for three main dishes. We can make either a hearty beef stroganoff, a zesty lemon garlic chicken, or a vegetarian butternut squash risotto. Any preferences?"

Sam considered for a moment. "The lemon garlic chicken sounds delicious. Let's go with that."

Rachel nodded approvingly. "Great choice. But first, any food allergies or preferences I should know about? And what does your husband usually enjoy?"

Sam's smile faltered slightly. "No allergies, but I should mention I'm recently divorced. It's just me now."

Rachel's eyes widened, a flush creeping up her neck. "Oh, I'm so sorry! I didn't mean to assume—"

"It's okay," Sam assured her, waving it off. "Really, it's not important."

Visibly relieved, Rachel launched into the lesson. "Right, let's get started on that chicken. We can make a quick orzo pasta salad to go along with it. We'll toss it with cherry tomatoes, feta, and a light vinaigrette."

They started butterflying and then pounding the chicken for even cooking. Rachel was quiet for a few moments before asking in a hesitant voice, "Was Dom like that with everybody last night?"

Sam looked up from her slicing and gave her a reassuring smile. "Believe me when I say that it wasn't only you. He was carping at everyone. You just missed it."

Rachel smiled back at her. "Okay, good. I mean, I'm sorry he was such a pill to everybody, but I'm glad I wasn't singled out. He came over to your house in that mood?"

"He did. We all figured Dom was having a bad day and taking it out on all of us. I don't know if it was something at work or something at home."

Rachel fidgeted with her apron for a moment. "When Dom stormed off to the terrace like that, I thought about following him out there. Have it out with him right then. But then I figured he wasn't exactly going to be reasonable when he was in that state of mind."

"Reasonable about what?"

Rachel colored a little. "With Dom working at the bank as some kind of head honcho, I thought the least he could do was to give me a loan to try and get the restaurant going again." She took a deep breath. "I know I'd said that I wouldn't take a loan from him, but that wasn't the truth. It was my pride talking. Anyway, instead of following Dom onto the terrace, I went to the restroom to wash my face, instead. I thought I might burst into tears and humiliate myself if I charged after Dom. The last thing I wanted to do was show any sign of weakness to him. I could imagine him mocking me for it."

Rachel looked like she was struggling to get in control of her emotions while recounting how she felt. To inject a lighter mood, Sam said, "How did you like the wallpaper in there? In the restroom, I mean."

"I loved it," Rachel said with a grin. "I mean, I love wallpaper in general. I know not everybody feels the same."

"You didn't think the monkeys were over the top?"

"No," said Rachel, "I thought they were adorable."

It was an interesting comment, considering there was no wallpaper of any kind in Sam's house.

"How well did you know Dom?" asked Sam. They were slicing lemons and mincing garlic now.

Rachel blinked at her. "Oh, I didn't know him at all. Not personally, I mean. He took some sort of umbrage at my restaurant and decided to ruin my life. Maybe he was bored."

"That must have made you furious."

Rachel was looking down at the lemon she was slicing. "It made me angry, of course. The worst part was that I wanted to get my anger out of my system, and I couldn't. I needed to rant at Dom, but I didn't know how to find him. Nora did, then."

"And Nora was a regular at the restaurant. Even when your parents owned it."

Rachel nodded. "Exactly. Anyway, I'm not the kind to bear grudges; that kind of bitterness can eat a person up from the inside. I did need to vent at Dom. I needed to get all my frustration out and let him know how badly he messed up my life. I knew that would make all my anger drain away." Rachel interrupted herself for a moment. "Okay, now we need to sear the chicken in that hot skillet we've prepped."

Sam said, "I'm still pretty new to town, and I never got the chance to eat at your restaurant. Tell me a little about it."

A fond look came across Rachel's features. "It was like home for me. I was so proud of that place."

"Your parents owned it before you took it over?"

"Well, sort of. They'd owned the building, but it was a totally different restaurant. It was a cozy little diner called 'The Blue Ridge Café' that was a favorite with the locals. Red and white checkered tablecloths, mismatched chairs, and the best biscuits and gravy in town. Dad would be at the grill from dawn, and Mom knew every customer by name."

"Sounds like it must have been a popular place," said Sam.

"Very. It was the kind of place where locals would sit around and gossip while Mom filled up their coffee cups. I grew up in the restaurant, like my sister did. When they passed away, within months of each other, I wanted to honor their legacy while bringing something new to Sunset Ridge. I called it Elevation. We kept a few of Dad's classic dishes, like his famous country-fried steak, but I also introduced more refined Southern cuisine. Like shrimp and grits with a smoky Tasso ham reduction, or a deconstructed peach cobbler with lavender ice cream. The property had sat empty for years, and I could get loans to start up the restaurant." She paused to direct Sam on the orzo pasta salad for a minute.

"What did the locals think about the change?" asked Sam.

"At first, there was some hesitation," Rachel admitted. "Although, once they tasted the food, most people embraced it. We became the go-to spot for special occasions, and even started attracting food critics from bigger cities." Her face fell. "That is, until Dom started his campaign against us."

They worked in companionable silence for a couple of minutes. Rachel still seemed to have both her restaurant and Dom's murder on her mind. "I hope you don't mind talking about this stuff," she said slowly. "I guess I'm trying to work through it all. I'm kind of shocked that he's really gone."

"And you didn't get the chance to actually give him a piece of your mind?"

Rachel nodded. "Right. I mean, maybe I let him have it just a little. But nothing like what I wanted to tell him. I feel like that chance was ripped away from me." She sighed. "I shouldn't even be thinking that way. I should be feeling bad for his poor wife."

"How exactly did Dom ruin your business?" asked Sam slowly. "It sounds like it was fairly direct."

Rachel's jaw tightened as she aggressively minced the garlic. "It was insidious. At first, it was only a few negative online reviews. Then, I started noticing canceled reservations. Regular customers stopped coming in. I'd overhear whispers about food poisoning or health code violations—all completely false."

She paused, taking a deep breath. "The final blow came when a food critic from Atlanta was scheduled to visit. Somehow, Dom found out." Rachel's voice cracked. "He paid off my produce supplier to deliver subpar ingredients that day. The review was scathing. After that, it was like the whole town turned its back on us."

Sam's eyes widened. "That's awful, Rachel. I'm so sorry you had to go through that."

Rachel nodded, blinking back tears. "The worst part was watching my staff—people who'd become like family—lose their jobs. Some of them had worked for my parents, you know? It wasn't just my dream that Dom crushed, it was theirs too."

"Why would he do something like that?"

Rachel shrugged again. "Who knows? I think he was somebody who enjoyed having a sense of power over others. It didn't help that he was such an influential person in Sunset Ridge and knew so many people. Plus, when the business started tapering off after he'd written awful online reviews and done word-of-mouth damage, I went to his bank for a loan, and he denied it."

Sam shook her head. No wonder Rachel had been furious. It sounded like Dom had completely sabotaged her business for no reason at all.

Rachel walked Sam through de-glazing the pan with white wine and chicken broth. She pulled cream out of the fridge and reduced the sauce.

Sam said in an offhand manner, "Do you have any idea who might have done this to Dom?"

Rachel snorted as she added fresh herbs and a squeeze of lemon to the dish. "The cops probably think it was me. I mean, don't I seem like a likely candidate to you? From what they can see, I likely had all the reason in the world to murder Dom."

"And you were saying you were in the restroom during that time. Did anyone see you go in there? Just thinking that a solid alibi would definitely help the police leave you alone. They were asking me where everyone was, and I frankly had no idea." Again, Sam thought about the fact that Rachel had clearly lied about being in the bathroom. There were certainly no monkeys on the wallpaper there.

Rachel said, "You didn't know where your guests were because you were being a good hostess and seeing after everyone. But no, it wasn't the type of party where you could have an alibi unless his death happened while everybody was at the table. We were all milling around while he was outside sulking or whatever he was doing out there."

Like getting murdered. Sam said, "Is there anybody you think might have had something to gain from his death?"

Rachel considered this. "Maybe Olivia. Although she looked like she was in awful shape after she found out Dom had died."

Sam thought back to Olivia's pale face, her trembling hands. Then her vacant stare. She needed to check in on her friend today and see how she was holding up.

Rachel continued, "Olivia seemed really protective of her brother, from what I've seen. The three of them had come into the restaurant a couple of times before it closed. Dom was always picking on the brother. I can't remember what his name is."

"Jason."

"Jason, right," said Rachel. "He seemed like a nice guy. And he was pretty concerned about Olivia after Dom's death. Maybe Olivia flew off the handle at Dom because he was picking on Jason." She paused. "I also saw Olivia with an unguarded look on her face after Dom died. Her expression was definitely one of relief. Just for a second."

Sam said, "I'd imagine Olivia had a lot of mixed feelings. It couldn't have been easy living with Dom."

"No. I can't even imagine. He was a pain in the neck, from everything I'd seen." Rachel plated a small amount of the food. "Want to try some?"

Sam felt like they'd cooked enough to feed a small army. It would take her a week to eat all the food by herself. She decided she'd take some over for Jason and Olivia later. She sat down and tried the salad and the chicken. "Wow, this is really good."

Rachel chuckled. "You sound surprised."

"I guess I haven't had anything terrific lately."

Rachel shook her head. "Your food last night was wonderful. You're an excellent cook."

"Thanks. I guess, cooking for myself, my meals have been a lot more pedestrian lately. Aside from last night, of course. Do you think we can pack the rest of it up? I'm going to run it by for Olivia and Jason later. Unless you want some for yourself?"

"It's all for you," said Rachel with a smile. "That's sweet of you to bring food to the Stantons. And here I am calling Olivia a killer."

"Oh, we were just speculating. It's hard to imagine anybody could have done such a thing, isn't it? Especially with all of us right there."

They chatted for a few more minutes before Sam left with the food and a promise to see Rachel later.

Chapter Nine

With the food from Rachel's cooking class in hand, Sam headed over to Olivia's house. It was an enormous house with an immaculate lawn and not a particularly personable feel to it. She couldn't help but wonder if Olivia planned on staying put or moving. It was a big place for one person, especially since Jason would presumably move out after he found work.

Sam walked down the long front walk and rang the doorbell. Jason answered the door. He looked very serious and tired. Sam gave him a small smile. "I brought some food for you and Olivia. Nothing from last night," she quickly added, as if having the association with the fateful dinner party might taint the offering. "I was at a cooking class with Rachel Reynolds, and we made this together."

She couldn't think why she was rambling so much. That wasn't really like her. Perhaps she had some residual feelings of guilt from last night. If she hadn't hosted that party, Dom would still be alive.

"Thank you," said Jason. "That's really kind of you. If you're trying to catch Olivia, I'm afraid she's out. She's over at the funeral home making plans for the service."

Jason looked tired and a little strung out. Or maybe hungover. She could see there were a lot of cardboard boxes and trash bags in the foyer and into what she could see of the living room.

Jason turned to follow her gaze. "Yeah, I thought it would help Olivia move forward if we started going through Dom's things. I got up early this morning and got moving on it."

It seemed more like a testament to Jason's dislike for Dom. The man had only died the night before.

"What did Olivia say?"

Jason looked rueful. "Actually, she was real conflicted about it. But when she woke up this morning and saw what I'd done, she seemed glad I was doing it. So while she's out of the house, I decided to get another big chunk of it done." He paused. "Hey, while you're here, did you talk more to the cops last night? After everyone had left?"

Sam shook her head. "I got an overnight bag together and Arlo and I went to a hotel."

"Got it. I wondered if you'd gotten any kind of feel from them as to who they think might have done this. I mean, obviously, it was somebody at the party. I'm worried they think it's Olivia. Or me, of course. Don't they usually believe the spouse did it?" He gave a short laugh. "Or the brother-in-law."

"I don't have any idea. I got the feeling they were going through their usual protocol when something like that happens. Interviewing people, securing the scene, and just going down a checklist. Did you or Olivia have an alibi for the police, when Dom was out on the terrace?" Although Sam had the feeling that everyone was in the same boat. The guests were coming and going in and out of rooms after dessert was over and while Dom was on the terrace. As far as she knew, no one had been in a prolonged conversation with another guest for the duration of Dom's time outside.

Jason said, "Like I told the cops, my goal was to stay out of Dom's way. I was well-aware Dom considered me a target. But I had to stay on his good side because I relied on him to give me a place to stay. I didn't want to rock the boat. So no alibi for me. I was in and out of the living room and dining room, getting more beer." He made a face. "I wanted to be more sober than Dom, but I definitely needed something to deal with the tension in there."

"I'm sorry it was such a rough dinner party for everybody. I didn't realize the dynamics were going to be so bad when I came up with the guest list."

Jason shook his head. "Don't worry about that. You didn't know what kind of mood Dom was going to be in when he showed up. Nobody did. I don't think Dom had a lot of control over his emotions, so even *he* probably didn't know what kind of mood he would be in."

"Had he been very erratic lately? With his moods, I mean?"

Jason snorted. "That guy was always erratic. He wasn't crazy about me, ever, of course, but he could be very tender to Olivia or awful to her. Believe me, I'm glad he's gone. He made Olivia's life complicated and miserable most of the time. Olivia didn't want me to get involved, though. She said she and Dom were working through whatever problems they had. But I couldn't stand by and watch him be ugly to her. As my big sister, she always looked after me when I was little. I wanted to make sure I looked out for her now." He paused. "Of course, I guess she's still looking after me, isn't she? I'm the one living in her house."

Sam said carefully, "How's the job market looking?"

"Not so great. But I'll find something. It takes time and persistence. On the bright side, it's given Olivia and me time to catch up with each other. Just like the old days."

From his expression, though, Sam wondered if he was telling the whole truth. "What was it like when the two of you were growing up? It sounds like you must have been really close."

Jason's face and voice softened at the memories. "We were. Still are, of course. We didn't have the easiest time growing up, though. Although we always had each other. Our family didn't have a lot of money. Olivia was a hard worker and always tried hard at school. She wanted to get ahead and get out of the house. She was motivated, is what I'm trying to say."

"Well, she definitely turned out well," said Sam with a smile.

Jason nodded. "Better than the rest of us. I was always the screw-up at school."

"I'm sure that wasn't true."

"Unfortunately, it was totally true. I was the class clown and the one acting out. I was the one trying to get attention. The house we grew up in was very stressful. Our dad was an alcoholic with a temper, and those two things shouldn't go together. Mom was depressed and not really functional. I mean, she wasn't cleaning the house, cooking meals, or running errands. Neither one of them would sign tests or report cards. Olivia did all the things they didn't do."

"That must have been tough on her."

"For sure," said Jason. "Olivia would cook for me and make sure I was in clean clothes for school. She kept track of when it was PE day and sent me to school with my gym bag. When Olivia went off to college, things got a lot worse. Our dad finally left, then Mom was barely getting out of bed in the morning. I wasn't well-equipped enough to take care of myself."

Sam asked, "How did Olivia and Dom meet?"

"In college. She was head-over-heels in love with him. The problem was, there was something about Dom that reminded me of Dad. It made me worried. I couldn't believe Olivia, smart as she is, would fall for somebody who was so much like our father."

"Was Dom always a heavy drinker?" asked Sam.

"Not usually," said Jason slowly. "But he was the same kind of personality type as Dad. Controlling. Cruel. I could see the similarities right away, but Olivia seemed completely blind to them. I did talk to her, before she married Dom. She didn't see the similarity at all. Over time, though, she caught on. I knew it wouldn't be long before Dom's true nature started coming out. And now, here we are, suspects in his murder."

"Can you think of anyone else at the party who might have done it? A better suspect than either you or Olivia? Did anybody stand out?"

"Now that you mention it," said Jason, "I thought Vanessa was acting odd. You know she and Dom were having an affair."

Sam raised her eyebrows. She certainly did not know they were having an affair. Her guest list for the dinner party would have been quite different if she had known. "I had no idea."

"Yeah, I don't think anybody really did. I heard Dom on the phone recently, hissing at somebody and telling them they weren't supposed to call him on that phone."

"And that was Vanessa?" Sam asked.

She must have sounded doubtful because Jason quickly added, "Must have been. Because I heard an in-person argument between Dom and Vanessa not long after that. Dom didn't realize I was in the house; he thought I'd gone out with Olivia."

"What was the argument about?"

Jason said, "Dom wanted to end things and Vanessa didn't, as far as I could tell. Anyway, it was clear they were an item. I was trying to decide whether to tell Olivia or not. After all, I'm kind of in a precarious position. If my sister had confronted Dom about the affair, he might have kicked both of us out of the house. And neither one of us has a job."

"You said Vanessa was acting oddly at the party?"

"That's right," said Jason. "She was a fidgety mess. She also was avoiding eye contact with everybody."

"I put that down to being new to the neighborhood and not really knowing many people there."

Jason shrugged. "I guess if you didn't know the background between Dom and Vanessa, that could be an explanation. But I've been thinking about it. I didn't see Vanessa during some of the time. She could have been outside, shoving Dom down the stairs. Maybe she went outside to talk to him and try to ask him to continue the affair. Then she got mad and gave him a push."

"That's a possibility. But she also might just have gone to the restroom. Or stepped outside the front door to get some air. Nobody at the party so far has had an alibi as to where they were when Dom was on the terrace."

Jason sighed. "That's what makes it frustrating. It should be easier to clear Olivia's and my name than it actually is."

Sam said, "I know. Maybe things will change soon. Well, I'm sure it will turn out all right. I'll keep my ears open for job openings. I'd better head on out."

"Thanks for the food, Sam."

Sam headed back home, thinking everything over. Jason was right—he and Olivia were the obvious suspects. Out of everyone at the party, Dom had been roughest on Jason. But Rachel made a pretty good suspect herself. And now, knowing that Vanessa had been romantically involved with Dom, it seemed like she might have her reasons for getting angry with Dom, too.

Chapter Ten

When Sam got to the top of her driveway, she saw a young boy standing by the garage door, waiting for her to arrive. Sam gave him a smile, but inside her heart sank. It was Franklin Smith. She'd given him a ride to school not long ago when he'd missed the bus. She wondered what he might have missed this time. Definitely not school, since it was a Saturday. Soccer practice? Was it even soccer season? It was November.

"How's everything going, Franklin?" asked Sam as she stepped out of the car.

He was a small, wiry boy who looked younger than his actual age of probably eight or nine. He had a mop of unruly sandy brown hair that never seemed to stay in place. His face was sprinkled with freckles across his nose and cheeks, and his bright green eyes always sparkled with curiosity or mischief. He wore clothes that were slightly too big for him, as if he was constantly waiting to grow into them.

"It's okay, I guess," said Franklin in a lackadaisical manner, scuffing his shoe against the driveway. Then, perking up, he asked, "Where's Arlo?"

Sam couldn't help but smile at the sudden enthusiasm in his voice. "He's inside. Did you want to see him?"

Franklin nodded seriously, as if this was a matter of utmost importance.

"Okay, well, let's head inside," Sam said, fishing for her keys.

They did, and Arlo joyfully greeted them as if he'd been waiting all day for this moment. His tail wagged so hard his whole body shook, and he pranced around them, alternating between sniffing Franklin's shoes and looking up at Sam with adoring eyes.

"Arlo is a great dog," said Franklin solemnly.

"Yes, he is." The boy was looking so earnest that Sam was beginning to wonder if he was going to demand ownership of Arlo.

"How about if I walk him?" asked Franklin, tilting his head as he looked at Sam.

Sam frowned. "Does your mom know where you are?"

"Oh, she wanted me out of the house because my video game was driving her crazy," Franklin said with a shrug, as if this was a perfectly normal explanation.

Sam promptly looked up his mother's number in the homeowners' directory and texted her, letting her know both where her son was and what he wanted to do with Arlo. She was apparently delighted Franklin was proposing some form of exercise and quickly agreed to the plan.

Sam put Arlo's harness and leash on, taking extra care to make sure everything was secure. She knelt down at Franklin's level, her voice gentle but firm. "Now, I need you to promise me a few things, okay? Always walk against traffic so you can see cars coming. Be very, very careful at intersections. And if Arlo gets too excited or starts pulling too hard, stop walking until he calms down. Can you do that for me?"

Franklin nodded solemnly, his face a picture of determination. "I promise, Ms. Sam. I'll take good care of Arlo."

With a last pat on Arlo's head and a reassuring smile to Franklin, Sam watched as the odd pair set out on their adventure, Arlo's tail wagging happily and Franklin chattering away to his canine companion.

About ten minutes later, Sam got a phone call from Aiden. Her heart made a little flip when she saw Aiden's name on the screen.

"Hey there. Just wanted to make sure Arlo hadn't been dognapped by a very young offender."

Sam smiled, feeling the blush creep up her neck again at the sound of his voice. "Thanks for checking. Franklin showed up wanting to walk Arlo. I got the okay from his mom. I mean, Franklin's mom, not Arlo's." She cringed at her awkward joke, but Aiden's chuckle on the other end made her relax.

"Arlo looked like he was having fun," said Aiden. "His tongue was hanging out, and he and Franklin were going at a pretty fast pace. I saw them zip past my house."

"That doesn't surprise me. I understand Franklin might be as much in need of exercise as Arlo is."

Aiden chuckled again, the sound warming Sam more than she cared to admit. Then, his tone softening, he asked, "How are you holding up after last night? Were you able to get any sleep?"

The concern in his voice touched her. "Surprisingly, I slept like a rock. I was thinking it was going to be one of those nights where I tossed and turned. Maybe the beer was enough to push me over the edge where I could actually catch a little sleep." Sam frowned as another call buzzed in. "Hold on, looks like I'm getting a call."

She pulled back the phone to look at it. It was her mother. She pressed her lips together, a familiar tension creeping into her shoulders. "It's my mom."

"I'll let you go."

"No, it's okay," said Sam. "I'm not going to pick up."

"You don't want to answer it?" asked Aiden slowly.

"We're estranged, unfortunately. Although Mother doesn't seem to understand the rules of estrangement."

There was a pause on the other end, and Sam could almost picture Aiden processing this information. When he spoke again, his voice was gentle. "That sounds complicated. I'm here if you ever want to talk about it."

Sam felt a rush of gratitude at his offer, even if she wasn't ready to take him up on it just yet. "Thanks, Aiden. I appreciate that."

Sam was relieved as Aiden smoothly changed the subject. "So, any exciting plans for your Saturday? Besides supervising impromptu dog walks, of course."

She chuckled, grateful for the shift in tone. "Oh, you know, the usual thrilling HOA president duties. I've got a riveting evening of reviewing landscaping proposals ahead of me."

"Sounds like a real page-turner," Aiden teased. "Don't forget to take breaks for snacks and dramatic reenactments."

"I'll try to contain my enthusiasm," Sam replied, grinning. "What about you? Any big weekend plans?"

"Well, I was thinking about tackling that leaky faucet in my kitchen. It's been my arch-nemesis for weeks now."

"Ooh, a showdown with household plumbing. Now that's living on the edge."

They both laughed, and Sam felt the last of her tension from earlier melting away. She was still smiling minutes later when they hung up.

It had been such a full day that when Franklin came back with Arlo, Sam didn't have the energy to do anything else but put her feet up and relax the rest of the day. While she was resting, though, she took a look at the local agility club offerings that the woman at the dog park had mentioned to her. They had a website that looked like it was well-updated. Sure enough, there was a meet-up the next day—Sunday afternoon. Right now, Sam felt too worn out to even think about it. But then, glancing over at Arlo, who was still looking wistfully out the glass storm door, she decided she'd try to make it.

The next morning, Sam slept in a little. When she opened her eyes and saw daylight outside, it startled her. It was almost always dark when she woke up. The events of Friday night must have lingered into last night, too.

Arlo was on the bed with her, looking at her with curiosity. She rubbed him. "I know. You probably were about to feel for my pulse, weren't you? It's pretty late to be getting up."

She yawned, pulled on a robe, and set about letting Arlo out and putting breakfast out for him. Then she went back into her room to put on exercise clothes, which was her usual routine. But then, she was clearly out of her usual routine this morning.

After doing a particularly unenergetic and uninspired exercise program, Sam ate breakfast, then got showered and dressed. Arlo would want his walk soon.

By the time she and Arlo came back from the walk, she saw someone waiting at her front door. It wasn't Franklin this time, but an adult. As they walked closer, she realized it was Vanessa Martin.

Chapter Eleven

Vanessa jumped when Sam called out to her. Then she turned, giving Sam a tight smile. "That's why you weren't answering the doorbell."

"Yes. Just walking Arlo." Sam fished her key out of her pocket. "Want to come inside?"

Arlo seemed to realize that this particular time, the visitor at the door was not there to visit him. He walked in, drank water, and curled up on his bed, watching Sam and Vanessa with interest as they walked into the living room.

"Can I get you a cup of coffee? Or maybe a glass of water?" asked Sam.

Vanessa shook her head. "I'm fine, thanks." She paused. "I'm sorry for barging in like this. I just realized I might be messing up your morning."

Sam smiled at her. "Oh, I was perfectly capable of messing up my own morning today. I overslept."

Vanessa gave a vague nod. Then she cleared her throat. "I was hoping I could talk with you about the party. The murder." She said the last word as if it left an awful taste in her mouth.

"The police have been talking to me a lot. Have they had another interview with you?"

"Not yet, but I'm sure they will." Sam wasn't actually sure of any such thing. She didn't have any negative history with Dom. There wasn't much of a motive there except for Dom being snide about her cooking.

Vanessa looked a little less tense. "Do you think they're coming back around to speak with everyone?"

"I'd imagine that's part of their protocol. They'd want to be sure and get as much information as they can." Sam saw Vanessa was looking tense again. "Are you sure I can't get you anything? Are you all right?"

Vanessa said roughly, "No, I'm fine, thank you. I haven't had any sleep the last couple of nights, worrying about this."

"I'm sorry. I'd have definitely rethought the guest list if I'd known it was going to be such a combative night."

Vanessa said in a low voice, "You see, Dom and I were having an affair." She flushed. "I can't believe I'm telling you this. I haven't talked about this with anyone. I think that's my problem right now—I can't keep these worries to myself anymore. If I don't tell someone, I'm going to lose my mind."

Vanessa clearly didn't know that word about the affair was out, at least to one person. Jason clearly knew about it, since he'd mentioned it to Sam yesterday. But he'd said he hadn't told his sister about it.

"I see," said Sam, trying to sound as if she was hearing the information for the first time.

"I'm sorry to be dumping this on you." Vanessa looked as if it had occurred to her that perhaps it was a lot to be burdening someone with. But then, Sam figured Vanessa was new to the neighborhood and didn't really have anyone to confide in. Although she wasn't new to Sunset Ridge. Did she not have other friends to discuss this with?

Vanessa seemed to read Sam's mind. Her flush deepened. "I felt like I wanted to tell you about this because I think the police are going to see me as a suspect. I didn't want to talk with my friends about it."

Sam nodded, and Vanessa continued. "I don't even know who told the cops about it. I definitely didn't. It was something that I never intended for anybody to know."

Sam thought again about Jason. She had the feeling she knew exactly how the police had found out about Dom's and Vanessa's affair. But then, Jason was trying to deflect police attention from Olivia. And himself.

"Did you have an alibi for the police?" Sam asked. "I mean, I know we were all in the house together, but could someone vouch for your whereabouts during the time Dom was outside? Derek, maybe?"

Vanessa gave a chilly laugh. "Derek? No. The police informed my husband about my affair with Dom. I guess they wanted to see his reaction and whether he looked surprised at hearing about it."

"The police think Derek knew about the affair and murdered Dom?"

Vanessa shrugged a thin shoulder. "Who knows what they think? But that's what I'm guessing. Anyway, suffice it to say that Derek isn't currently in the mood to give me an alibi. Even if he could." She sighed. "I took a business call outside for a few minutes. But not out the back," she added quickly. "I stepped outside the front door."

"What line of work are you in?"

Vanessa said, "I'm an interior designer. Sometimes I get client calls on the weekends or in the evenings. When you own your own business, that goes with the territory. So nobody had eyes on me the entire time." She gave a short, unhappy laugh. "You can see why I'm worried."

"And you're sure Derek didn't know anything about your affair with Dom?" asked Sam.

"I don't think so. But Derek doesn't show his emotions a lot. He's the kind of guy who keeps his feelings locked away. It's possible that he could have known, or at least guessed." She sighed. "We've had some tension in our marriage. Just for the last six months or so."

Sam said, "That's not uncommon."

"Did you and Chad have that kind of tension?"

Sam stiffened a little at Chad's name. She'd gotten used to people avoiding the topic. She felt pain piercing her at the mention. Especially since Vanessa had never even met Chad. It meant people had been talking about Chad. And Sam, too.

Vanessa must have noticed because she quickly said, "I'm so sorry. I shouldn't have said anything about Chad."

Sam smiled reassuringly at her. "It's okay. And you're right, we had a few moments of tension. But nothing big. Clearly, tension or lack of it is no real indicator of a problem in a marriage."

Vanessa looked relieved that Sam had given her a pass on the mention of Chad. She quickly got back on the topic of Dom. "Dom was such a mess Friday night. It must have been the alcohol; I could tell he'd been drinking a lot. I was worried he was going to reveal our affair to everybody."

Sam remembered Dom's overly familiar remarks to Vanessa. She had the feeling he might very well have revealed their affair, probably relishing the audience. No wonder the cops thought she was a suspect.

"I should never have started the affair with Dom. I don't know what I was thinking. He was so charming at first. He and I would often be home at the same time in the early afternoons—he apparently did a lot of remote work. And Derek would still be at school." Vanessa looked away. "Derek and I have had some financial struggles lately. Neither one of us makes much money, and I guess moving to our new house was a stretch for us. But we both really liked the neighborhood and loved the house."

Sam said, "I'm sure financial worries would have added some tension to your marriage."

"Exactly. It's just been a tough time. And I'll admit that I didn't grow up with money problems. I came from a pretty well-to-do family, had a great education, and enjoyed a career in the arts before I set out into design. It's been a real adjustment not having the money I'm used to." Vanessa made a face. "Sorry. That sounds bratty of me."

"It sounds like the truth."

"It is," said Vanessa. "Anyway, Dom and I started this ill-advised affair. He even offered to lend me money. I'm ashamed to say I took it. I never should have even considered doing that. And all the time, I had really conflicted feelings about Dom. He was never really kind to me, and having an affair took an emotional toll on me. I felt bad about Derek. Of course, during the party, I was horrified at the idea that Dom might come out and talk about our relationship. But I never would have killed him."

"Do you have any idea who might have?"

Vanessa said, "Maybe Rachel. After all, his negative reviews and bad-mouthing of her restaurant led to her business failing. I can totally see her wanting revenge on him. I know she was very proud of her restaurant."

"Are you and Rachel friends?"

Vanessa said, "She and I have known each other since we were kids, although we've never been very close."

"Oh, I didn't realize you grew up here."

Vanessa nodded. "Sure did. Left for college, but then came back to Sunset Ridge." She made a face. "Dom grew up here, too. And he was a bully back then. He really gave Rachel a hard time."

Sam frowned. Rachel had told her she didn't know Dom, aside from the negative reviews. "Dom was in school with you and Rachel?"

"That's right. I guess I should have realized that people don't really change. Yeah, Dom had grown up, but it didn't mean he'd become a nicer person. I should never have gotten involved with him." Vanessa shook her head, looking down at the floor. Arlo got up from his little bed and trotted over to lean against her. Vanessa gave a sob. "Oh my gosh, what a sweet dog."

"He's pretty empathetic," said Sam with a smile. Then she said slowly, "Are you planning on staying with Derek?"

"Well, if he'll forgive me for having an affair. And now, I guess, I've also made sure both Derek and me are suspects for murder. What a mess." Vanessa paused. "There was one thing I noticed at the party. There were a few minutes when Dom wasn't taking target practice at everybody. He and Alfred were having what I suppose they thought was a private conversation." She gave a wry smile. "Of course, it didn't end up being private. Alfred was asking for more time and Dom was turning him down."

Sam felt her heart sink. She loved Mandy and Alfred and hated to think that either of them could be mixed up in Dom's murder. "So Alfred borrowed money from Dom?"

"It sure sounded that way. I could tell from Dom's tone that he wasn't being very nice. He could definitely be a cruel man."

Sam said, "But banks are full of red tape. It's not as if Dom would have a lot of leeway in terms of paying back a loan."

"I got the impression it was probably a private loan. Like the kind he gave me." Vanessa gave Arlo one more rub, then stood. She gave Sam a smile. "Thanks for letting me drop in on you like this. I feel better, talking about it."

Sam stood up, too. "Of course. Anytime, Vanessa."

Chapter Twelve

After Vanessa left, Sam sat down again in the living room with a notebook and a pen. Her mind felt like it needed a brain dump—there was just too much information crammed into it. When she felt like that, there was nothing better than a list.

She wrote the names of everyone who had been at her ill-fated dinner party. Then, beside them, she wrote their connection to Dom, or why they might have wanted Dom out of the way.

As she carefully thought it through, she felt slightly traitorous to her guests. But, after all, one of them appeared to be a killer. No one thought a stranger had scaled the fence to her property, ascended the terrace, and thrown Dom down the stone stairs.

After a few minutes, her list looked like this:

Rachel Reynolds: *Angry with Dom for her restaurant's closure. Lied about not knowing Dom—according to Vanessa, grew up with Dom and was bullied by him at school. Rachel also lied about being in the restroom while Dom was on the terrace.*

Olivia Stanton: *Abused by Dom? Bullied by Dom, certainly. Protective of her younger brother, Jason, who Dom was harassing at dinner.*

Jason Barnes: *Living with Dom and Olivia, unemployed. Dom was persecuting him at dinner, telling him all the ways he didn't measure up.*

Derek Martin: *Knew about his wife's affair with Dom?*

Vanessa Martin: *Had affair with Dom. Worried Dom was going to expose the affair? End affair? Borrowed money from Dom to help alleviate financial problems.*

Alfred and Mandy Jones: *Alfred borrowed money from Dom? A private loan, like Vanessa's was?*

Nora Snodwick: *No idea. She felt very protective toward Olivia and Rachel, however. Would she even be strong enough to push Dom down a staircase?*

Sam tapped her pen on the paper. It wouldn't do—she'd have to reach out to Nora. Nora was the kind of person you wanted to have on your side in the neighborhood. Having her be in a snit at Sam for not inviting her to the dinner party wasn't a good thing.

Sam steeled herself, then made the phone call. She was about to leave a message when Nora finally picked up.

"Sam," said Nora in a cool voice.

Sam forced a cheerful note into her own voice. "Hi there, Nora. How are you holding up after Friday night?"

Nora sniffed. "Well, I'm holding up better than Dom, that's for sure."

Sam cleared her throat. "I wanted to invite you to lunch, if you haven't already eaten. My treat, of course. It's the least I can do." Sam didn't explain further. That way, Nora could take it that Sam was apologizing for not inviting Nora to the dinner party to begin with, or for basically hosting a murder during the event.

Nora seemed to thaw out. "I haven't eaten yet. But I do have various dietary concerns to consider."

"Why don't you pick the place?"

Nora immediately said, "Let's go to the Highland Grill."

Naturally, Nora had picked the most exclusive lunch spot in town. "Perfect," said Sam. "What time should I pick you up?"

"How about now?" asked Nora before firmly replacing the phone receiver.

Sam took a prophylactic aspirin before leaving the house. Nora could be stressful to be around, at least for Sam. Maybe it was the way she found fault in so many things, and people, around her. Or maybe it was the fact that Nora seemed to see right through Sam. She might realize that maybe Sam didn't have her life as perfectly arranged as it appeared. Of course, probably many people thought that now, considering Sam's ex-husband was in prison.

Nora was waiting at the bottom of her driveway, a judgmental expression on her face. She carefully climbed into the backseat.

"Oh, Nora. Why don't you sit in the passenger seat, next to me?"

Nora sniffed. "No thank you. The safest place in the car is the backseat. Everyone knows that."

Sam knew it as well, but somehow hadn't imagined her toting Nora around town like a limo driver. Still, the purpose of the outing was to appease Nora and appease Nora she would.

Sam supposed it was easier to apologize to Nora while she was out of view. "I wanted to let you know I was sorry for not inviting you to the dinner party Friday."

Nora huffed.

"I was trying to get back on the horse, you know." Sam paused. "I haven't entertained since everything happened with Chad. So my plan was to make things as easy as possible for me. I kept my headcount low and tried choosing people who got along well."

"*That* was an abject failure," said Nora coolly.

"Yes. Yes, it was."

Nora said, "Well, I'm not going to apologize for bringing Rachel there. She needed the opportunity to tell Dom Stanton exactly what he'd done to her. He was so cavalier—not answering her calls or coming to the door when Rachel went by! Absurd. I saw his car over at your place and knew it would be the perfect chance to tell him off."

Nora sounded very grandmotherly about the whole thing. Sam said, "I think you were acquainted with Rachel's family? And the original restaurant?"

"Of course I was. They were *friends*, not acquaintances. And I couldn't stand having Dom treat her so arrogantly, especially after what he did."

Judging from Nora's tone, she was still furious. Could *Nora* have pushed Dom down the stairs? Sam hadn't originally thought she'd be able to, but Nora was surprisingly hale and hardy. Plus, Dom had been drinking quite a bit and was unsteady on his feet. It might not have taken much to unbalance him at all.

They reached the restaurant, and Sam started the search for parking. Although Sunset Ridge wasn't a large town, the downtown spots were usually grabbed by tourists who were in the area for hiking, camping, zip lining, fishing, or lake sports. Nora directed Sam from the backseat.

"There's a spot! Right there!" said Nora in a peremptory tone.

"It's parallel parking. I'm not really a fan of parallel parking." Plus, it was the worst sort of parallel parking. The kind where someone was already in front and behind the parking place.

"For heaven's sake," growled Nora. "Pull over and let me drive. I'll get into the spot."

Sam, however, had no intention of allowing Nora to do that. She squared her shoulders. "No, I can do it."

And she did. But it took over five minutes of backing up, pulling forward, gauging, and retrying. Finally, Nora hopped out of the car and barked instructions on which way to turn the wheel until Sam got into the parking place as well as possible.

"Well, that was harrowing," said Nora, looking rattled.

"I did mention that I wasn't much of a parallel parker." Sam took a deep breath and pasted a smile on her face. "Lunch?"

Chapter Thirteen

Despite the way their lunch date started, things became much more amiable as they walked in. Nora relaxed when she was seated in the dining room. Highland Grill was a historic inn and had lovely wood beams on the ceiling, wonderful wooden floors, and lots of charm. The hostess, a young woman with a welcoming smile, led them to a table near one window overlooking downtown. Nora settled into her seat with a relaxed sigh.

The menu was extensive, even for lunch. Their server, a polite young man named Troy, appeared with a wine list. Nora waved away the list with a dismissive hand. "Just water for me, thank you. And don't bring me any of those lemon wedges. They're teeming with bacteria."

Although Sam felt a glass of wine would really help take the edge off, she didn't want to risk Nora's displeasure. "I'll have an iced tea, please. No lemon," she quickly added. Nora gave her an approving nod.

The Highland Grill apparently prided itself on using locally sourced ingredients. It took both women some time to delve into the menu and decide. Nora finally settled on the grilled salmon with a side of roasted vegetables and quinoa. "I need to look out for my heart," she muttered. "Only heart-healthy stuff for me."

Sam opted for the herb-crusted chicken breast with a warm Farro salad. As they waited for their meals, Sam broached the subject of Dom's death. "I know Friday night was difficult for everyone. How are you really doing?"

Nora's face clouded over momentarily. "Well, it certainly wasn't how I expected the evening to go. Dom Stanton may have been a thorn in my side, but I wouldn't have wished that on him." She paused, then added with a hint of her usual sharpness, "Though I can't say I'm surprised someone finally did him in."

"Do you have any thoughts about who might have done this?"

"Well, it certainly wasn't Olivia. The very idea!" Nora glared at Sam as if Sam had suggested otherwise.

"No, of course not."

"I should say not," said Nora, not looking in the least mollified. "Nor Rachel. They're both wonderful girls who have put up with more than their fair share."

Sam knew Nora had her favorites. She was also rapidly coming to the conclusion that she herself wasn't one of them. "I'm sure Rachel had nothing to do with it."

"Naturally. So that leaves a bunch of men and that Vanessa woman," said Nora. Vanessa clearly wasn't a favorite, either.

"I don't really know Vanessa very well," confided Sam, hoping Nora would gossip a bit in return. Nora loved a good gossip.

"Then why did you invite her to your dinner party?" asked Nora acerbically.

"Well, she and Derek are new to the neighborhood. I thought it would be nice for them to meet other neighbors. And for me to get to know them better."

Nora seemed satisfied by this. "I suppose so. I do know Vanessa, but not from the neighborhood. I know her because she grew up here. A rather unpleasant little girl, I always thought."

"She mentioned she'd grown up in some comfort."

"Yes, the family had money," said Nora. "Not that they knew what to do with it. Reckless people, all of them."

"Reckless?"

"Nouveau riche," said Nora with a sniff. "They wasted their money on frivolous pursuits."

"Did they run through it all?"

Nora said, "I suppose they must have, because they ended up downsizing. But that was after Vanessa had already left for college."

"Why do you think she was unpleasant?"

Nora said, "She was sort of full of herself. Snobby. Not that she really had anything to be snobby about."

"She seems fine now."

Nora looked as if she might debate the point, but then shrugged. "If you say so. I didn't talk with her on Friday. But then, Vanessa didn't make any effort to come speak with me, either."

Sam guessed that was because Nora was impossible to get along with. No wonder Vanessa avoided her.

"What about the others? Any thoughts on them?" asked Sam.

Nora shrugged again. "Who knows? I don't know Derek or Jason well. Derek was very polite when I saw him while I was out walking Precious one day. He complimented Precious's tutu. He has a new one that's especially adorable. It has a rich, royal tulle at the base that really stands out against his brindle coat. Layered over that are shimmering silver stars."

"He must look gorgeous in it," said Sam. She managed, as always, to hide her smile at the thought of a male pit bull in a tutu.

"He does. Anyway, that's all I know about Derek—that he complimented Precious. Who else was there? Oh, right. Naturally, Alfred and Mandy are very nice people, although I do think they struggle a bit with money."

Their conversation was interrupted by the arrival of their meals. The presentation was impeccable, each plate a work of art. Nora's salmon was perfectly grilled, its skin crispy and golden, nestled atop a colorful medley of roasted vegetables. Sam's chicken looked equally enticing, the herb crust giving off a fragrant aroma that made her mouth water.

As they ate, their conversation drifted to lighter topics. "Tell me a little about Sunset Ridge. You seem to know quite a bit about the area," said Sam, buttering Nora up. So Nora regaled Sam with tales of Sunset Ridge's history, peppering her stories with gossip about long-time residents. Sam found herself genuinely enjoying Nora's company, the older woman's caustic wit now more amusing than abrasive.

Nora stopped her monologue to ask, "What do *you* make of Sunset Ridge? As a fairly new resident still?"

Sam could tell from Nora's tone that she wasn't going to accept any criticism of the little mountain town. Fortunately, Sam had none to give. "It's gorgeous," she said. "Like it's been plucked from a postcard. I love Main Street with the boutiques in restaurants inside all the restored Victorian buildings. And the gazebo right at the heart of the town, in the middle of the park."

Nora nodded, seeming satisfied by her response. "Have you been to any of the events there? In the park where the gazebo is?"

"Not yet." This was mostly due to Sam's retreat from society after Chad's betrayal.

"You should. It's hosted everything from bluegrass concerts to artisan markets. Oh, and another must-see spot is the historic Ridgeline Theater."

Sam asked, "Is that the art-deco building downtown?"

"Exactly. It was lovingly restored some years ago. Anyway, it shows all sorts of independent films and has an annual film festival that brings cinephiles from all over."

As they finished their meals, Nora dabbed her mouth with her napkin and fixed Sam with a penetrating gaze. "You know, my dear, I may have misjudged you. You're not half bad, for a newcomer."

Sam felt a smile pull at her lips at the unexpected compliment. "Thanks. I've really enjoyed our lunch."

As they prepared to leave, Sam noticed Nora eyeing the dessert menu wistfully. On impulse, Sam said, "Why don't we split a slice of that lemon meringue pie? I understand it's their specialty." And although Sam had made meringues, she hadn't actually been able to eat any of them.

Nora's eyes lit up. "Well, I suppose a small indulgence won't hurt. But don't you dare tell my doctor."

As they savored each bite of the meringue, Sam felt a sense of accomplishment. She might not have won Nora over completely, but it was a start.

As they left the restaurant, Nora touched Sam's arm lightly. "Thank you for lunch, dear. It was very pleasant." Coming from Nora, it was high praise indeed.

Chapter Fourteen

When Sam got back home, she did a few chores around the house, then put her feet up for a few minutes. She was startled forty minutes later to find she'd fallen asleep. She wasn't much of a napper, since she usually felt very groggy when she woke up, as if she'd somehow plunged directly into REM sleep. This time, though, she felt somewhat rested. Arlo, who was dozing next to her on the sofa, was making little snoring sounds.

Sam said, "Do we want to try out the agility training thing?"

Arlo's eyes opened, and he looked quizzically at Sam.

"It could be a lot of fun. Or it could be lame. We could try it and see."

Arlo cocked his head to one side, trying to decipher what Sam was talking about.

"If we don't enjoy it, or don't like the people, we can always make an excuse and leave early. Or sneak out."

Arlo grinned at Sam. He wasn't entirely sure what he was saying, but he sensed they were about to do something. Something out in the car. And going out in the car with Sam was one of Arlo's favorite things to do.

It wasn't a long drive to the canine center. She was glad she'd mapped it on her phone, because it was indeed in the middle of a field, as the woman at the dog park had mentioned. But the field was fenced in and had a rustic DIY charm to it. There were obstacles spread across the field, with clear paths between them for running. There were shade trees around the edges and a simple shelter where the club members were gathered in folding chairs. Sam also spotted lots of water bowls for the dogs.

Sam had somehow imagined the canine center was an indoor facility, although she wasn't sure where she'd come up with that. She'd thought she might sit quietly with Arlo at the very back of a room, watch the proceedings, and then quietly slip away at the end if she wasn't interested in the activity.

This was completely impossible, however. She was greeted immediately by a whirlwind of a woman with wild, curly red hair and a megawatt smile. "Welcome, welcome! I'm Ginny, and this little tornado is Pixie." She gestured to a small, wiry Jack Russell terrier who was doing excited circles around her feet.

"Hi, I'm Sam, and this is Arlo," Sam managed, overwhelmed by the enthusiastic welcome.

"Oh, Arlo is adorable. What a sweetheart," Ginny cooed, bending down to let Arlo sniff her hand. "Come on, let me introduce you to everyone."

Although everyone had been under the shelter when she'd driven up, they'd migrated over to the field. And, before Sam could protest, she was ushered onto the field, filled with an assortment of colorful obstacles—jumps, tunnels, seesaws, a tire hoop, weave poles, and things Sam couldn't even name. People and dogs of all shapes and sizes were scattered around, chatting and playing.

"Everyone, this is Sam and Arlo." Ginny announced loudly, causing several heads to turn their way. Sam felt her cheeks flush, but managed a small wave.

A lanky man with salt-and-pepper hair approached them, a sleek border collie at his heels. "Hey there, I'm Dave, and this is Rocket. Don't let Ginny scare you off; she's just really excited about new people."

Sam laughed, feeling herself relax a bit. "Nice to meet you both. Rocket looks like he lives up to his name."

Dave grinned. "Oh, you have no idea. This boy could probably run circles around all of us combined."

As they chatted, Sam noticed a familiar face across the way. It was the woman from the dog park—what was her name again? Lisa? Laura?

"Lucy!" Ginny called out, waving the woman over. "Come meet Sam and Arlo." After making this order, she headed off to greet another newcomer.

Lucy made her way over, her whippet padding along beside her. "Hi Sam, good to see you again," she said with a warm smile. "I see Arlo convinced you to give agility a try?"

Sam chuckled. "I think it was more Arlo's enthusiasm for the park that convinced me. I figured he might enjoy something like this."

"Oh, he'll love it," Lucy assured her. "Ziggy here was a bit unsure at first, but now he can't get enough of it." She patted the whippet's head affectionately.

"Alright, folks," Ginny called out, clapping her hands. "Let's get this show on the road. Newbies, don't worry; we're doing some basic introductions today. No pressure."

Sam watched in amazement as dogs and their handlers navigated the course, some with graceful precision, others with endearing clumsiness. Dave and Rocket moved like a well-oiled machine, while Ginny and Pixie's run was more chaotic, but filled with joyous energy.

When it was Sam's turn to try a simple sequence with Arlo, she experienced a small flutter of nerves. "I have no idea what I'm doing," she admitted to Lucy, who was standing nearby.

"None of us did at first," Lucy reassured her. "Just have fun with it. Arlo will pick up on your energy."

The little dog looked up at her with those soulful eyes, tail wagging in anticipation.

"All right, buddy," Sam murmured, "let's show them what we've got."

She led Arlo to the start of a simple sequence, which was a low jump followed by a short tunnel. Simple enough, or so she thought.

"Whenever you're ready," Ginny called out cheerfully from the sidelines.

Sam took a deep breath, pointed to the jump, and said firmly, "Arlo, jump!"

Arlo tilted his head, gave her a quizzical look, then promptly sat down.

A ripple of good-natured laughter went through the gathered club members. Sam felt her cheeks flush.

"It's okay," Lucy called out. "First time jitters are totally normal for both of you!"

Sam nodded, trying to push down her embarrassment. She was used to excelling at everything she tried. This was humbling.

"Let's try again," she said, more to herself than to Arlo. "Jump!"

This time, Arlo stood up, wagged his tail . . . and walked around the jump.

Sam could feel her Type-A personality kicking into overdrive. There had to be a system, a method, a list she could make to master this.

"Hey," Dave said gently, coming over. "Why don't I show you a little trick?"

For the next few minutes, Dave demonstrated how to use treats to lure Arlo over the jump and through the tunnel. By the end of their first lesson, Arlo was cautiously completing the sequence, with only minor detours to sniff interesting spots on the grass.

Sam found herself making a mental list: *1. Buy treat pouch. 2. Research positive reinforcement techniques. 3. Set up mini agility course in the backyard.*

She looked down at Arlo, who was trotting along happily beside her, completely oblivious to her planning. "Look at you two!" Ginny said. "You're naturals."

As the session wound down, Sam chatted with Dave and Lucy, exchanging phone numbers and making plans to meet up for coffee and a "puppy playdate" at some point in the near future.

"So, think you'll be back next week?" Dave asked as they were packing up.

Sam looked down at Arlo, who was wagging his tail and looking up at her with those soulful eyes. She smiled. "You know what? I think we probably will."

When Sam arrived back home and drove into her garage, she found Arlo was knocked out asleep in the backseat. He gradually woke up, yawning twice.

"That was even more exercise than you got with Franklin," said Sam. "Let's go inside and get you supper."

Arlo perked up at the mention of supper. And soon, both Arlo and Sam were settled on the sofa again, watching television and relaxing after the events of the day.

Chapter Fifteen

The next morning, Sam woke up early for her volunteering at the community food bank. Usually, Olivia joined her on Mondays to organize and pack the donated food, but Sam guessed Olivia wouldn't feel up to it, conbsidering.

But she saw Olivia's car parked outside when Sam drove up to the Sunset Ridge Community Food Bank. It was a modest, single-story building on the outskirts of town with a faded brick exterior but a well-organized interior with long metal shelving units, each meticulously labeled and stocked with non-perishable foods. It also held a large walk-in cooler full of fresh produce and dairy items.

As Sam walked in, she saw Olivia was already hard at work in the sorting area. Olivia gave her a smile, and Sam reached out to hug her. "Hey there," said Sam. "I'm surprised to see you here today."

"Oh, I needed to get out of the house," said Olivia. "I've got to stay active or else my mind keeps straying back to Dom." She paused. "Thanks so much for the delicious dinner you brought for Jason and me. That was so thoughtful of you."

Sam started inspecting cans for damage, proper sealing, and expiration dates. "Well, Rachel invited me over for a free cooking class. The meal I brought over was what I made in the class. She felt bad about gatecrashing."

Olivia gave a short laugh. "Rachel picked the wrong party to gatecrash."

"Yeah, it's not every day you inadvertently become a murder suspect when you think you're attending a dinner party."

Olivia gave a gasping laugh, then kept going until tears trickled down her cheeks. "I'm sorry," she said.

"Don't be! You probably need a release valve for all the different emotions you're feeling. I can't imagine what you're going through right now."

Olivia started sorting donations into canned goods, dry goods, and personal care items. "Honestly, I'm not sure I can accurately identify all the different emotions I'm feeling, myself. It's been something of a rollercoaster." She glanced around to make sure they were still the only ones in the food bank. "The police seem very interested in what I was doing during the dinner party."

Sam gave her a reassuring smile. "Believe me, everyone I've talked to has said the same thing. Except for Nora. No one seems to think she's done it."

"Nora would be the perfect murderer. You can tell she's got a killer instinct. She does exactly what she wants to all the time with no repercussions. She could get away with murder easily."

Sam said, "Except she doesn't really have a motive, aside from the fact that she's very protective of both you and Rachel. I kept having the feeling that if she thought either of you were being threatened in any way, she'd step right in and do something about it."

Olivia sorted some more donations for a minute without speaking. Then she said, "You're right—she absolutely would. And Nora never did like Dom." She turned to look at Sam. "Do you really think the police are focusing on everybody right now? Not just me?"

"I'm sure of it."

Olivia breathed out a sigh. "That's good to hear. I've been thinking about how the police were focusing on me during the last murder, you know. I felt a sense of déjà vu."

"Remember, though, that time they suspected you and nothing came of it."

"That's true," said Olivia, sounding relieved. "Thanks, Sam. Maybe things will turn out all right. I didn't have a great alibi during the party. I couldn't even really remember what I'd done."

"Everyone else is in the same boat," said Sam. "It was a dinner party, so people were milling around, getting drinks, nibbling more on desserts, going to the restroom."

"Yes, but I couldn't even *tell* the cops what I was doing. I was so stressed out that it was like my brain stopped recording what was happening. I'm sure I gave them a terrible impression."

"I'm sorry," said Sam in a low voice. "I know Friday night wasn't easy on you—either before *or* after."

"No, it wasn't. Dom was in such a foul mood. Not even just a regular bad mood, but a *nasty* one, like he wanted to stir up mischief."

Sam reflected he had succeeded beyond his wildest hopes, if that was the case.

"I told the police I'd spent some time playing tug with Arlo. That was one thing I actually *did* remember. The sweet little guy came trotted up to me with his tug toy in his mouth. The funny thing was, he had this really sympathetic look on his face. Like he *knew* I was having a rough time. Arlo should be a therapy dog."

Sam chuckled. "He's a sweetheart, that's for sure. The thing is, I just got him involved in an agility course group. Not that he couldn't do both things, but there are only so many hours in the day."

"That sounds fun. Is he going to compete?"

Sam said, "It's way too early to tell. We went to our first meeting yesterday. We both had a great time."

"That's something. Let me know how it goes."

The two women worked quietly for a few minutes, both of them lost in their thoughts. They were now sorting the canned foods into more specific groupings of vegetables, fruits, and canned meats, then arranging them by expiration date on the metal shelves to make sure the older items were used first.

Finally, Olivia spoke again. "The sad thing is, I was so relieved when Dom stepped outside on your terrace. I thought maybe it was going to be the equivalent of 'time-out' where the cold air might clear his mind. That maybe he'd come back inside in a better mood. Or, if not, that at least we were all getting a break from him for a few minutes." She gave a small sob. "I know it sounds ridiculous that I miss him so much. I know I had that affair when I felt really low and disconnected from Dom. But I never wanted anything to happen to him."

Sam said firmly, "There's no right or wrong way to feel right now."

"Good," said Olivia, sniffing. "Because I feel so conflicted. I'm mourning Dom, but I'm also relieved he's gone. My life is easier in a lot of ways right now, I have to admit. Aside from planning Dom's service, of course. It's going to be in a couple of days."

"I'll be there. Is there anything I can do to help you out?" Sam's mind immediately started making a list of things she could help with.

Olivia smirked a little, as if she knew Sam was coming up with tactical approaches to helping with the service. "Maybe. I'm working on it." She quietly sorted for a few minutes. Then she said, "I can't stop replaying Friday night in my head. I didn't even know what Dom was talking about half the time. It makes me feel like I didn't know him all that well."

"Do you know much about him, growing up?"

Olivia shook her head. "Not really. Dom didn't like to talk about it much. I got the impression he ran with a kind of crazy crowd, though. And that he and his parents had a lot of stand-offs when he was a teenager."

"Are his parents still alive?"

Olivia looked sad. "His mom is gone, but his dad is still around. He's not in great shape, though. I had to tell him what had happened, and he looked devastated." She frowned. "Like I said, I can't seem to get past all the things Dom was saying Friday night. I didn't realize Dom had basically gotten Rachel's restaurant shut down. And I don't know what he was baiting Alfred about."

Sam noticed Olivia didn't say anything about Vanessa. Olivia's brother, Jason, might have said nothing to her about it. But hadn't the police? They'd have wanted to see Olivia's reaction to news of the affair, surely. Whether or not she looked surprised. And whether there might have been a flicker of guilt.

Olivia continued. "I don't know why Dom would have basically shut down Rachel's restaurant. Sometimes, it seemed like he could be incredibly cruel for no reason at all." She sighed. "Naturally, he was awful to Jason. Of course, Dom was *always* awful to him. I would never have suggested Jason move in with us, but he really had nowhere else to go. I couldn't just abandon him."

Her voice had a pleading note to it, as if hoping Sam saw her point of view. "Of course you couldn't. He's your little brother."

Olivia turned to give Sam a grateful look. "Exactly. You get it. Dom didn't, though. He was an only child, so he never realized how close you can get to a sibling. He also didn't get the fact that people can go through tough times. You can lose a job. You can have a tough time finding a new one. You can lose your housing."

"Dom had a privileged upbringing," said Sam.

"Right. And that influenced his viewpoint on everything. Dom had only known success and money and found it hard to relate to anyone who didn't have those things." Olivia put a few sorted items on the metal shelves. "The part that really bothered me was when he belittled Jason the way he did. Jason is doing the very best he can, no matter what Dom thought." Olivia paused. "So I wasn't surprised by Dom picking at Jason on Friday. But when he was goading Rachel and Alfred, it was definitely a surprise. And then . . . that stuff with Vanessa? It was more of a shock."

Olivia was now studiously not looking at Sam. She took a deep breath. "Dom was having an affair with Vanessa."

Sam didn't want to reveal that Jason had already told her about the phone conversation he'd overheard between Dom and Vanessa. Nor the in-person argument. And she certainly didn't want to say that Vanessa had admitted to the affair. So she carefully said, "I'm so sorry, Olivia."

Olivia bobbed her head. "Yeah. I didn't find out about it until the night of your party. I could tell by his manner toward her. I know I couldn't really be upset about the affair, considering I'd cheated on Dom, myself. Still, it really hurt. And, of course, the police somehow knew about it. Maybe Vanessa told them. Now the police are probably convinced I killed Dom because he was having an affair."

The women were quiet again for a minute while they worked and were deep in their own thoughts. Then Sam said, "Is there anyone you think has more motive than you do? Someone you could point out to the police?"

Olivia said wryly, "Well, the person who comes to mind had exactly the same motive I did, so I'm not sure it improves my position. Derek Martin."

"You think he knew about his wife's affair with Dom?"

Olivia said, "Considering how much Dom was revealing Friday night, he could very well have come to the same conclusion I did. I thought he was standing close to the kitchen door leading out to the terrace when you came back in after discovering Dom."

The problem with that theory was that lots of people had been in and out of the kitchen. There had been both food and beverages in there. Sam nodded. "It sounds like a possibility."

Olivia said, "Not to change the subject, but going back to the memorial service. Like I said, my head's all over the place. You're so great at planning and organizing things. Would you give me a hand?"

"Of course, I'd be happy to. Do you want to talk it through today? Or tomorrow?"

Olivia looked rueful. "Although I feel like I'd rather tackle it tomorrow, considering the service is going to be in a couple of days, we'd better figure it out today. Maybe late-afternoon? I might try to go for a hike this afternoon to clear my head."

"Sure, that sounds great."

The rest of the volunteer shift, Olivia and Sam stuck carefully to completely different, much lighter topics. Sam did her best to distract Olivia, which was the reason Olivia was on her shift to begin with. But the dark expression in her eyes never did clear completely away.

Chapter Sixteen

Olivia had told Sam to run by her house at four o'clock, so that was when Sam showed up. Sam, naturally, had a laptop bag with her, notebooks, and a pen, ready to help. But when Sam rang the doorbell, Jason was the one who answered.

"Hey there," he said with a smile. "Are you looking for Olivia?"

Sam nodded. "She asked me to give her a hand planning Dom's service."

Jason made a face. "That's a tough assignment. You're a good friend to help out with that. Dom wasn't a particularly religious man, so it's not like he had a favorite hymn or Bible verse. And poor Olivia is still having a hard time grappling with his death to begin with."

"I feel bad for her. She and I volunteered at the food bank together this morning. But by the end of our shift, she looked like she was feeling a little more upbeat."

Jason said, "Then you did a world of good for her. All I've been able to do is finish clearing out Dom's things." He stepped aside and showed Sam the entryway, which was now free of all the boxes that had been there the last time.

"Wow, you made a lot of progress."

"I was hoping if I got rid of some reminders of Dom, it would help Olivia deal with his death. But it's not exactly that easy," he said ruefully.

"May I talk with Olivia?"

Jason frowned. "Oh, I'm sorry. I didn't mention—she's out of the house."

That didn't seem right. Olivia was always punctual, and she was the one who'd set up the time for them to meet up. "That's funny. She asked me to be here at four o'clock."

"Huh. She must have lost track of the time. She told me she was heading out on a hike. She'll be back. Why don't you come inside and wait a few minutes?"

Sam's brow furrowed as she considered her response. "Has she been on the hike for a while? She'd mentioned to me that she was planning on going, but I didn't get the impression it was going to be a long one. And it's going to be dark soon." She texted Olivia and waited. There was no response.

She noticed for the first time that Jason appeared to have a glass in his hand. Sam could smell alcohol on his breath, too. Maybe that was why he was so laid back about Olivia's absence.

Jason was frowning now, looking up at the November sky as if suddenly realizing the sun wouldn't be out for long. "Okay," he said slowly. "That is kind of weird, actually."

"I don't want to over-react, but I feel like I should go check things out. Do you remember what trail Olivia said she'd be hiking on? I can look for her car in the parking lot." There was still no response from Olivia, but maybe she was out of cell phone range on the trail.

Jason looked like he was trying hard to remember what Olivia might have said. But he also seemed to have a lot of brain fog, possibly from whatever was in his glass. "I think she said she was going to hike the Rainbow Trail."

It was a well-known, well-maintained trail with a waterfall at the end. Sam nodded, already heading back to her car. "Got it. I'll text you and let you know."

"I'm coming with you," said Jason, hastily locking the door behind him.

Ordinarily, this would be fine, but of course Jason was a murder suspect, the same as they all were. On a Monday November evening at this time, the trail would probably be deserted. "Sure," she said. But to be on the same side, she texted Aiden. He should be back from teaching school by now—she really didn't want to bother Mandy, who would still be at work. And the idea of texting Nora made her shudder. She sent Aiden a brief message to say that they didn't really know where Olivia was and where she and Jason were heading, just in case.

Her phone pinged immediately as she climbed into the driver's seat. Sam checked to make sure it wasn't Olivia. It was Aiden, though, sounding concerned. She texted him back, saying she was about to start driving. Then she and Jason headed out.

The fading daylight and the accompanying cooler temperatures made Sam drive faster than she ordinarily would have.

Jason was still trying to talk himself into believing Olivia would be found safe and sound. "Maybe she lost track of time," he said again.

It was hard to lose track of time when you were losing daylight, though. Sam said, "I know. And maybe she's out of cell phone range."

This prompted Jason to pull his phone out of his pocket and dial his sister's number. It rang and rang, though. He left a message. Then, a few minutes later, he dialed again.

Finally, they reached the trailhead parking area. And there was Olivia's car. Jason groaned.

"Maybe she took a tumble on the trail and twisted her ankle or something," said Sam quickly. They stepped out of the car. The wind was picking up, and the temperatures were rapidly dropping with the sunset. Sam pulled out a heavy coat she kept in the trunk and put it on. There was also a pair of gloves carefully stashed in a bag, along with a knit cap.

Despite his anxiety, Jason stared. "Wow, you've got a whole emergency kit back here. Heavy clothes. A blanket. Flashlights."

Just the things a Type-A person would keep in their trunk. Sam said, "That reminds me. Let me grab the first-aid kit, just in case." She handed a flashlight to Jason and picked up a small daypack which had the first-aid kit in it.

Jason looked solemn again as they headed out onto the trail. The path was a mix of packed earth and loose gravel, with occasional protruding tree roots that became more treacherous as their visibility decreased. Small rocks and pebbles crunched underfoot, the sound seeming unnaturally loud in the surrounding quiet. Even louder were their calls as they shouted for Olivia.

As they walked up the mountain, the trail became steeper and narrower in places, with rocky outcroppings on one side and a sharp drop-off on the other. The fading light made it difficult to gauge the depth of these drop-offs, which added to the sense of unease Sam felt.

As they hiked, their flashlight beams cut through the growing darkness. The beams of light caught the occasional glint of animal eyes watching from the forest, quickly disappearing as they moved on.

About halfway up the trail, they came to a small clearing. The path widened slightly, offering a view of the valley below, now shrouded in deepening twilight. It was in this clearing that they made their grim discovery.

Their flashlights caught a flash of color—the bright purple of Olivia's hiking jacket. She lay motionless at the base of a large boulder, partially hidden by low-growing ferns.

Chapter Seventeen

"Olivia!" Jason cried out, rushing forward.

Sam quickly followed, her heart pounding. Olivia was sprawled in an unnatural position, her hiking pole lying nearby. There was no response to Jason's frantic calls.

Sam knelt beside Olivia, her fingers seeking a pulse at her neck. It was there, but weak and thready. Sam put her ear by Olivia's mouth. Her breathing was shallow and labored.

"We need help.

Jason's eyes were wild. "Is she going to be okay?"

"Let's get her help. Do you have a signal here?" Sam was looking at her phone. She hadn't had a connection for a few minutes.

Jason checked his phone. "No connection for me."

"I've got a bar. I'll give it a try."

Sam could somehow get through. She quickly reported what happened and where they were. Then she hung up.

"Stay with us, Olivia," Sam murmured, keeping pressure on the head wound with her jacket. The fabric was already soaked through, dark in the fading light. Her first aid training kicked in - keep the victim still, maintain body temperature, monitor breathing.

"Should we move her?" Jason's voice cracked with panic.

"No," Sam said firmly. "With a head injury, we can't risk it. But here." She guided his hands to hold the makeshift compress. "Keep pressure right here while I check her."

Sam ran through her assessment, speaking aloud to keep Jason focused. "She's breathing—it's shallow but regular. Her pulse is weak but there." The November wind was picking up, and shock was a real concern.

"She's so cold," Jason said, his voice tight with fear.

"I have an emergency blanket in my pack," Sam remembered, quickly pulling out the silvery thermal blanket. Together, they carefully wrapped it around Olivia, trying to conserve what body heat they could.

"Talk to her, Jason," Sam encouraged. "Let her know you're here."

Jason leaned closer to his sister. "Hey, Liv. You're going to be okay. Remember all the times you took care of me? Now it's my turn to look after you."

Sam noticed Olivia's fingers twitching. "Good. Keep talking. I think she can hear you."

She checked Olivia's pupils with the flashlight from her phone and noticed her uneven dilation. Not good. The wound was still bleeding despite the pressure. Where was that ambulance?

The sound of sirens echoed in the distance. Sam squeezed Olivia's hand. "Help's almost here. Just hold on."

"Her breathing's changed," Jason said suddenly, panic rising in his voice.

Sam leaned down, listening intently. The breathing was more labored now. "Keep talking to her. We need to keep her stable."

A minute later, Sam heard someone calling her name. She recognized the voice. "Aiden?" she asked.

Jason looked confused. "What's he doing here?"

"I thought someone should know where we were. Just in case."

A beam of light suddenly cut through the darkness, accompanied by the sound of hurried footsteps on the gravel path. Sam and Jason turned to see Aiden approaching, his tall frame and broad shoulders silhouetted against the fading twilight.

As he drew closer, Sam's flashlight illuminated his features. Aiden's black hair was tousled from the wind, and his green eyes were alert and focused. He was dressed practically for the temperature and impromptu hike, wearing a dark-colored fleece jacket over a flannel shirt, sturdy jeans, and hiking boots. A small backpack was slung over one shoulder.

Aiden said quietly, "What happened?"

In an undertone, Sam quickly caught him up.

"You think it was foul play?" asked Aiden.

"Maybe," said Sam. "The underbrush looked disturbed, like there might have been a struggle of some sort. The flashlight showed scuff marks, too. I don't know if that was from Olivia, or other hikers, but I'm sure the cops will want to take a look."

There was a sound from Jason, and Aiden and Sam turned back toward him. Aiden reached into his pack and pulled out another jacket, laying it over Olivia.

"You okay?" Aiden asked Jason.

A tear trickled down Jason's face. "She's all the family I had left, man. I can't believe this is happening." He gave a short laugh. "And besides worrying about her making it, I'm also being totally selfish and thinking of myself."

"What do you mean?" asked Sam.

Jason shrugged. "The cops are going to be all over me now. Especially with all the money problems I've had. First Dom dies. Then what if something happens to Olivia? Her estate is all going to me."

Sam and Aiden exchanged a quick look. Aiden said, "You know what's in Olivia's will?"

"Sure. She told me when she married Dom that they'd gotten updated wills. She said she was leaving everything to Dom and vice-versa. But that, if anything happened to both of them, I was going to get everything, unless they had kids." He put his head back in his hands. "I'm screwed."

Sam said, "Hey, the police are still looking at everybody. There were plenty of people who were suspects in Dom's death."

"Yeah, but not Olivia's. Who would want to murder Olivia?" Jason asked the question as if really wanting to know the answer.

"Maybe somebody who thought she knew who killed Dom," said Aiden quietly.

"Olivia didn't know who murdered Dom! She was just as lost as the rest of us." Jason took a deep breath, trying to calm himself down. "Look. It's totally true that I've been dealing with all kinds of money problems and stress. Lots of personal challenges. Losing my job put me in the hole financially, of course. That meant I lost my apartment. Then I lost my girlfriend at the same time—I guess she didn't want to stick around with somebody who was unemployed." He paused. "I've been struggling with alcohol, too. Using it as a crutch when I shouldn't have. I haven't felt very good about myself, lately."

Sam said, "I hope you weren't putting stock into anything Dom was saying about you. He was obviously trying to annoy you."

Jason gave a short laugh. "Well, he did that, all right. Dom knew exactly how to get under my skin. But I could have dealt with that forever. What I didn't like was when he was picking on Olivia. That would really make me mad." He paused. "I thought I was pretty composed during the dinner party, though. Considering what he was saying, I mean."

Sam nodded. "You were handling him really well."

"I'm also not a very confrontational guy, especially not in a social setting. I wanted to keep the situation from escalating any further." He grimaced. "Of course, *that* didn't happen. The evening ended with a murder."

Aiden said slowly, "It must have been really challenging living in the same house with Dom. Of course, I didn't arrive at Sam's house until after Dom's death, but from what I understand, he was in rare form."

The sirens were now much closer. They must have made it to the parking lot below.

"Yeah, Dom was a mess Friday night. The drinking definitely didn't help. I was incredibly frustrated with him. I wished he'd stayed at home. But he was stoked up. He wanted to take on the world, and that's what he did."

Sam said, "Was there anybody you thought might have attacked Olivia?"

"Well, last time I mentioned Vanessa, since Dom was having that affair with her and acted like he wanted to blab about it. Or maybe Dom wanted to end their affair. Maybe Vanessa thought Olivia knew something and needed to get rid of her."

Aiden asked, "Has Olivia seemed secretive lately? Or deep in thought?"

"Yeah, I guess she has, actually. I kind of figured it was because of the way Dom was acting. Then, after Dom died, I attributed it to her feeling really conflicted over him being dead. But maybe Olivia did know something I didn't realize. I wanted her to confide in me, but she didn't." He rubbed his face. "Maybe Olivia didn't want to worry me. Maybe she thought I had too much on *my* mind and didn't want to add anything else. I wish she had."

They could hear voices making their way up the trail.

Jason said, "There was one thing I've been thinking about. Dom apparently lent Alfred money. I don't know what it was for. But it wasn't a bank loan—it was personal. It's been a few weeks ago, but Dom was toying with Alfred on the phone about it. Like a fat cat with a mouse." He shook his head. "I really like Alfred. He and Mandy have been a couple of people who actually made me feel like I belonged in the neighborhood, even if I'm living there with my sister."

His voice hitched on the word, and he took a few moments to settle himself down again. Then he said, "I'd hate it to be Alfred. He's a really decent guy, and he's worth a dozen Doms. But maybe it's something the police should know."

Now they could hear the EMTs coming up the trail.

"Over here!" Aiden shouted as flashlight beams cut through the growing darkness.

The EMTs emerged from the darkness, equipment in hand, their movements quick but controlled. The lead paramedic, a woman with close-cropped gray hair, took charge immediately.

"I'm Sarah. How long has she been unconscious?" she asked, already kneeling beside Olivia.

"We found her maybe fifteen minutes ago," Sam said, quickly moving back to give them room. "Olivia hasn't responded, but her breathing and pulse have been steady until just now."

"Good catch with the thermal blanket," Sarah noted, efficiently attaching monitors. "BP's 90 over 60, pulse 120. Pupils unequal." Her partner was already starting an IV line.

"O2 stats dropping," he reported. "85 percent."

"Let's get her on oxygen," Sarah decided, pulling out a mask. "Watch that neck; we need a collar before we move her."

Jason hovered nearby, his face gray. "Is she going to make it?"

"We're going to take good care of her," Sarah assured him, her voice kind but professional. "But we need to move fast. Are you riding with us?"

"I'm her brother," Jason managed. "I'll go with you." He turned to Sam. "I'll Uber back home later on."

Getting Olivia down the trail was a careful choreography of emergency personnel. The stretcher had been specially designed for trail rescues, with all-terrain wheels, but the darkness and steep patches made every step treacherous.

"Watch that root," called one of the rescue team members. "Careful around this bend."

Sam followed behind, holding her flashlight steady to help illuminate the path. The beam caught the glint of medical equipment, the reflective strips on the EMTs' uniforms, the thermal blanket still wrapped around Olivia.

"BP's dropping again," Sarah announced from beside the stretcher. Even while moving, she kept constant watch on the monitors. "Push another bolus of saline."

They had to stop twice, once when the heart monitor started alarming, and again when Olivia's breathing became more labored. Each time, Sam watched the medical team work with precise efficiency, stabilizing her enough to continue the journey down.

"Almost to the ambulance," Sarah encouraged them. "Hang in there, Olivia."

The ambulance waited in the parking lot, emergency lights painting the trees in rhythmic flashes of red and white. The team transferred Olivia from the trail stretcher to the ambulance gurney with practiced coordination.

Jason climbed into the ambulance, looking lost among the medical equipment. Sarah was already calling ahead to the hospital: "Trauma team alert. 35-year-old female, severe head trauma."

There were flashing blue lights entering the parking lot, and Jason looked grim as he saw them. Then an EMT slammed the doors shut, and they were on their way.

Lieutenant Phillips got out of his car, as did the uniformed officers.

"I'm going to need someone to show me where Olivia was found," Phillips said solemnly. He glanced at Aiden. "Did you go to the location?"

Aiden nodded. "I'll show you where it is."

"If you can just show the uniformed guys. I'm going to have a word with Ms. Prescott for a few minutes, so she can fill me in."

Aiden gave Sam a questioning look, as if to make sure she was okay. She gave him a brief nod and he set out to guide the cops to the site.

The detective looked tired, but focused. "Okay. Ms. Prescott, I understand you were the one who initiated the search. Can you tell me what prompted your concern?"

Sam filled him in on the appointment Sam and Olivia had to plan Dom's service, her concerns about Olivia's lateness and the approaching darkness. She felt Phillips's keen gaze on her. He asked her again about her relationship with Olivia, how Jason ended up going with her to the trail, and what she'd seen there.

By the time Sam had wrapped up the story, exhaustion really set in. She wrapped her arms around herself.

Phillips said, "I'll get in touch if I have any further questions. But for now, you should try to get home and get some rest. And warm up." He stepped away to speak with a uniformed officer who was returning to report to Phillips. Aiden was right behind the cop.

Sam waited for Aiden to give Phillips a brief statement. Then he joined her.

Sam said, "Thanks for coming out tonight. It's not every day you have to set out into the dark and cold to check on a friend. At least, I *hope* it's not every day."

Aiden said, "I wanted to. I was worried when I got your text, especially considering the chill." He looked at her gloves, coat, and hat and gave a small grin. "I forgot who I was dealing with."

"Hmm? Oh, the clothes. I keep warm stuff in my car just in case I break down on a cold night."

Aiden said, "Well, it certainly came in handy tonight." He glanced over at the mobile command unit. "Jason seems like a great guy. I didn't *think* he would be dangerous, but I didn't want to take the chance."

"Yeah, that's the way I felt, too. That's why I wanted to let you know where I was and who I was with. I thought it might be a good idea to cover my bases." Sam looked over at the command unit, too. She sighed. "I feel really bad for him. I know having Olivia hanging on the brink like this has got to be incredibly stressful for Jason."

"They seem very close," said Aiden with a nod. He saw Sam shiver and said, "Hey, you need to get back home. I'll follow you."

But Phillips called him back for another question. Aiden reluctantly said, "I'll check in with you later," as he walked off to join the policeman.

Sam drove home, her mind racing despite her exhaustion. The house seemed eerily quiet when she walked in, even with Arlo's joyful greeting. She needed a hot shower to wash away the events of the evening, but first, she dropped onto the sofa, pulling Arlo close.

"What a night, buddy," she whispered into his fur. Her phone buzzed with a text from Aiden letting her know he'd made it home safely and reminding her to get some rest. She smiled faintly.

The shower could wait a few more minutes. Right now, she just needed to sit here with her dog, trying not to think about Olivia lying unconscious in that hospital bed, fighting for her life. Trying not to think about who might have wanted her dead. And whether they might try again.

Chapter Eighteen

After a night of tossing and turning, Sam gave up on sleeping altogether. She rose early, and called Jason.

"How is she?"

Jason sounded exhausted. "She's hanging in there, Sam. But they've put her in a coma. A medically-induced coma."

He sounded so worried that Sam immediately said, "I think they do those a lot, don't they? Doesn't it reduce brain swelling?"

"That's what they said," said Jason flatly. "Which reduces pressure. They said something about giving her brain tissue time to heal."

"Were the doctors able to give a prognosis?"

"They said it's too early to tell." Jason paused for a moment, then said, "Hey Sam, I forgot to tell you last night how much I appreciate you taking Olivia's absence seriously."

Sam started to brush this off, but Jason continued. "No, seriously. I'd been drinking. My head wasn't really in the right place. You were a great friend to Olivia. If you hadn't insisted on setting out after Olivia, she'd be dead right now. It's a good thing she wasn't up on the mountain waiting for *me* to rescue her." He gave a harsh laugh.

"You were with me," said Sam firmly. "You were the one who spoke to Olivia up there, who got her to respond. You're the one at her bedside right now."

Jason paused again, then said quietly. "Thank you. For everything." He hung up.

Sam exercised, ate breakfast, and then set out into the yard to do some yardwork and try to work out the events of the previous evening.

She was dead-heading the roses with a battery-powered hedge trimmer when she heard a squawking sound. She turned off the trimmer to see Nora there with a panicky look on her face. She was walking Precious, who was looking at her owner with a curious expression.

"Don't do it!" said Nora.

"Pardon?"

"Don't murder the roses!" said Nora. "You should be using handheld pruners. That's not the way to deadhead your plants."

Sam gave her a wry smile. "Got it. Well, the problem is there are many of them. I thought the quicker way to handle them would be to use the trimmer."

"Quicker is not always better," said Nora in a huffy voice.

Sam put the trimmer down, mostly because Nora was so obviously offended by it. She realized she should tell the old woman about Olivia. She was so fond of her, and it wouldn't be good for her to overhear gossip when she wasn't prepared. She cleared her throat. "Why don't you and Precious come in the house for a few minutes?"

"What? We're on a walk," said Nora slowly, as if Sam hadn't quite grasped the concept of walking a dog.

"Yes, of course you are. But could you? I wanted to talk with you for a minute."

Now Nora was curious. "Okay," she said cautiously.

"I'll meet you at the gate. It's over there."

Nora and Precious came into the yard. "You could just tell me here," said Nora, sounding grumpy.

But that was precisely what Sam didn't want to do. The last thing she wanted was for Nora to lose her balance in her yard after hearing bad news.

"It's a little too chilly for me," she said hesitantly.

"You were out here doing yardwork!"

Sam said, "Yes, but that was when I was moving around. If I'm still, I get cold."

Nora muttered something under her breath about people with poor constitutions, but followed Sam inside.

Arlo joyfully greeted Precious, who Nora had taken off her leash. The dogs had met during neighborhood walks and had seemed congenial enough when both were leashed. Sam was relieved to see they got along as well when they were off-leash.

"How about a hot cup of coffee?" suggested Sam.

Nora scowled at her. "How about you tell me what's going on? Otherwise, I'm going to think this is an elaborate ruse for you to sell me something. You don't peddle life insurance or something, do you?"

Sam shook her head. "No, I don't work, actually."

Nora sniffed, looking around her curiously at the lovely furnishings in the large home. "Nice gig if you can get it."

"I sold an app," said Sam with a self-conscious shrug.

"I have no idea what you're talking about. And, if you try and shed light on the subject, I suspect I'll be even more in the dark. Now, onto what you were going to tell me. I don't need coffee nor anything else."

Sam motioned for Nora to sit down, and the old woman did, frowning.

Sam took a deep breath. "I wanted to let you know that Olivia got badly hurt last night. She's in the hospital in a medically-induced coma."

Despite trying to be gentle, Nora immediately went pale. Her hand went up to grip her throat. "No."

"I'm so sorry, Nora. I know you really care about Olivia. But you needed to know."

Nora croaked, "What happened? Was it an accident? Did she fall down the stairs or something?"

Sam shook her head. "I'm sorry, Nora. The police are treating it as an attack."

Nora's mouth trembled. Then she said, "Tell me everything."

So Sam did. Nora made scoffing sounds at the mention of hiking. She listened intently as Sam talked about the approaching darkness, the cold temperatures, and how she and Jason found Olivia.

"How is Jason?" asked Nora.

"He's very upset. I talked to him earlier, and he sounded absolutely exhausted. He's at her bedside. I understand Olivia is really all he has."

Nora said in a brusque voice, "Yes, and not just financially, either. You can tell Olivia was almost like a mom to him, despite the fact there isn't that much age difference between them."

Precious, hearing something in his owner's voice, abandoned playing with Arlo to come over and lean comfortingly against Nora's leg. She reached down to rub him.

Sam said, "Can I get you something to drink now? Coffee? Tea? Water?"

"How about a bourbon and ginger ale?" asked Nora, her voice a bit trembly.

"Coming right up," said Sam, heading with relief to the kitchen and leaving Nora to have a couple of minutes to think.

Sam was heading back to the living room with the drink in her hand when Nora's phone started ringing. Nora looked at her phone and immediately answered it. "Rachel? Oh, not well at all. I just got some terrible news." She listened for a moment. "I'm over at Sam's house. Come on over."

It occurred to Sam that this was the second time Nora had gotten Rachel to come over to Sam's house. This time, though, she didn't mind in the slightest. A few minutes later, the doorbell rang, and Arlo announced to the room that there was someone there. Precious joined in to reiterate the point. Sam hurried to answer the door.

Rachel gave her an apologetic look at dropping in unexpectedly again. "Sorry. Is Nora here?"

"I'm in here, dear!" said Nora, her voice wavering.

"Are you okay?" asked Rachel. "Are you feeling well?"

"No, because my heart is hurting. Sam, tell Rachel what you told me."

Sam recounted what had happened the night before while Rachel watched with wide eyes.

"I can't believe it," said Rachel slowly. "First Dom dies, then his wife is attacked."

Nora frowned. "You don't think Jason is in danger too, do you? What is this world coming to?"

Sam said, "I'm sure Jason is taking care to be safe. I can't imagine someone is trying to eliminate the entire family."

"Then why?" demanded Nora, spreading her hands out wide. "Why would somebody try to kill Olivia?"

"I'm wondering if maybe she knew something about who murdered Dom," said Sam slowly. "That would explain why someone felt desperate enough to do this."

Nora looked over at Rachel. "This will fire up the police again, won't it?"

Rachel nodded, closing her eyes briefly. "They'll probably want to talk to everybody from the party again. I just wish this was over."

Nora barked, "Do you have an alibi? A good one for last night?"

"No. I made a few phone calls, looking to see if anyone needed a cook for their restaurant. Then I ran an errand."

"When was that?" asked Nora.

"Maybe three o'clock? Three-thirty?"

It definitely didn't seem like a strong alibi. Nora apparently didn't think so, either.

"That's too spotty," she growled.

Rachel looked even more alarmed than she had before. "But I don't have any reason to try to murder Olivia. I didn't have any bad feelings toward her at all. She had nothing to do with the restaurant's closure and obviously had no control over her husband at all."

Nora shrugged. "Doesn't really matter, in the cops' eyes." She was still looking doubtfully at Rachel. "Okay. How's the job search going? You know I think you should open another restaurant instead of working for somebody else."

Nora clearly thought highly of her own opinion. She stated it in a non-negotiable voice.

Rachel said in a cheerful voice, "Well, working for yourself is tough, Nora. I'm not saying there aren't a lot of positives. You get to be your own boss. The problem is . . . you get to be your own boss. And when you're your own boss, you don't go as easy on yourself as you would with other employees."

Nora clucked. "You shouldn't have been a workaholic."

"The problem is that there's always so much to do and only so many hours in the day. You've got to order food, manage people, work on the books. It's never-ending. And if your business isn't doing well, you're responsible. Not the kitchen staff."

Sam said, "It sounds like a huge responsibility."

"It is. Because if your restaurant is doing poorly, you're hurting your staff, too—not just yourself."

Nora said, "Well, this time you know exactly why your business failed. Because of that Dom Stanton. That's why I think you should open your restaurant again. He's not around anymore to cause you trouble."

"There's the matter of getting loans," said Rachel gently. "I know you liked eating there, and I loved serving you there. You were one of my most loyal customers. But I'm thinking that ship might have sailed."

Nora looked very displeased at hearing this information. But Sam was curious. Rachel sounded almost laid-back about the restaurant's closure. Did this mean she really *didn't* have much of a motive to murder Dom?

Rachel continued, "And, you know, I'm feeling optimistic about my future now. Before, I was so busy that it was hard for me to see the forest for the trees."

"Forest? Trees? What on earth are you talking about, Rachel?" asked Nora.

"I'm saying it's hard to look at the big picture, your career, when you're focusing so much on the day-to-day stuff. Maybe the restaurant closing was a sign I should try a different path. Maybe I don't need to be in the food industry at all. Maybe I need to figure out something completely different.

Nora muttered something under her breath. Sam smiled at Rachel. "That sounds like a great idea. Maybe this break will give you time to think."

"Thanks. Yeah, at first, I jumped right into looking for restaurant work. But now, I'm wondering if I should get with a life coach or something. Maybe they can help me discover other interests." Rachel stopped. "Hey, I'm sorry about being so upbeat right now. I somehow forgot about Olivia. I know how close Nora is to her. Do you know her well, Sam?"

"We're friends. Olivia and I volunteer together and hang out some, too."

Rachel nodded. "I felt sorry for Olivia, especially Friday night. I could tell how humiliated she felt because of how Dom was acting." She paused. "As bad as it sounds, I've hoped Dom's death is an opportunity for Olivia to take her life in a new direction, too. She always seemed like she was under Dom's thumb."

Nora nodded vigorously, her wizened face scrunching up. "Under his thumb? That's putting it mildly. That poor girl was practically a prisoner in her own home."

Sam raised an eyebrow. "Really? How so?"

"Oh, I could give you a list as long as my arm," Nora said, waving her hand dismissively. "For one, Dom controlled every penny that came into that house. Olivia couldn't even buy herself a new dress without his say-so."

Rachel's eyes widened. "That's awful. The poor woman."

Nora continued, her voice getting more animated. "And don't get me started on how he treated her at neighborhood functions. Remember last year's Fourth of July picnic? Dom spent the whole time parading Olivia around like some trophy, then snapped at her for talking too much to the Hendersons."

Sam frowned. "I wasn't here for that, but it sounds terrible."

"Terrible doesn't begin to cover it," Nora huffed. "And let's not forget how he'd always interrupt her or talk over her at HOA meetings. It was like he couldn't stand the idea of Olivia having thoughts of her own."

Sam shook her head. "I feel awful for not noticing all this before."

Nora's eyes softened a bit. "Well, Olivia was good at putting on a brave face. But living next door, I saw more than most." She leaned in, lowering her voice. "There were nights I'd hear them arguing through the walls. Dom's voice booming, Olivia's voice all quiet and shaky. It broke my heart, I tell you."

Sam felt a chill run down her spine. She'd known things weren't great between Olivia and Dom, but hearing these details made it all seem so much worse.

Nora turned to Rachel again. Her voice was kinder now. "Speaking of putting on a brave face, you're quite good at that yourself. I know you're trying to keeping a stiff upper lip, too. Good for you for trying to work through this mess. But you can't fool me. I know exactly how upset you were about your restaurant. It's me, remember? It was your family's place. Your heritage."

At Nora's tone, Rachel stiffened and blinked rapidly a few times.

"I don't want to make you cry," said Nora in alarm. "Don't do that."

Sam hid a smile. Nora seemed to think she could control people's emotions, even by the force of her will alone.

Rachel took a deep breath. "Okay. You know me pretty well, Nora. Of course I was upset. For one thing, Dom totally ruined my professional reputation. It's a small town, so if I want a job here, I need to rebuild that. Who's going to hire me if they believe the lies he told?"

It was almost like a dam had burst, and Rachel's worries were spilling out.

"No one is going to believe what that man said," said Nora crisply. "Everyone knew he was a liar."

Rachel said wryly, "Whether we want to believe it or not, Dom was a very influential man in town. He managed to make my restaurant close down, remember? People listened to him. But I've been trying to do some networking locally. I'm going to participate in some industry events, too. Maybe something will come of it. And, if it doesn't, I can try another line of business, like I was saying."

Nora's face had darkened as Rachel outlined how Dom's actions had affected her. "Are you doing self-care?" she demanded. "Everybody says it's very important to do self-care."

"I'm trying. I have an app that guides me through meditation."

Nora looked as if she might be a little suspicious about meditation. "All right. You're eating well? Sleeping well?"

"Eating well? Yes. Sleeping well? No. But it's been a little crazy lately, you know? Dom's murder and the investigation? But I've got good sleep hygiene normally."

Nora grunted at this. "Okay. What needs to happen is for the police to figure out what's going on here. Why aren't they out doing their jobs? Now Dom is dead and Olivia is in the hospital."

Sam said, "I think they're trying. I'm sure they'll find out who's behind this soon. Rachel, do you have any thoughts about who could have done it?"

Rachel sighed. "Well, last time I talked with you about this, I thought Olivia might have been involved."

Nora hissed.

"I know," said Rachel. "I'm ashamed of myself. I put myself in Olivia's shoes and thought I'd want to kill Dom if I were her. Now I'm not sure what to think."

Nora cut in. "I know what *I* think. I think it's that brother. He led Sam right to Olivia on the hiking trail."

Sam shook her head. "That's not how it happened."

"You don't know for sure! You might have felt like the two of you discovered her together, but it could have been totally different. If Olivia dies, he gets all that money! And we all know the financial trouble he's having."

Rachel said, "Aren't Jason and his sister really close, though? Do you think he'd kill her over money?"

"Of course!" said Nora. "Because it's money. Maybe he was secretly envious over Olivia and her lifestyle. It could have been eating him up inside. Then he saw his chance when she set out for that hike."

Sam said, "Jason couldn't have been too envious over Olivia. He saw up-close what her life was like. It sounds like Dom was making Olivia's life miserable from what you were saying, Nora. Do you really think he could attack his sister?"

"Well, I'm not totally sure," said Nora in a huff. "But some people lose their minds in the heat of the moment."

"But that's the thing—it wasn't the heat of the moment. If Jason followed his sister up the mountain, he had plenty of time to think about it."

Nora said, "Yes, but when there's a lot of money on the table, it can change people's morals and priorities." She looked at Sam closely. "What do you think happened? You're the one who was there."

"It doesn't mean I really know anything, though."

Nora glared at her. "You must have *opinions*. Or you might have heard things. Come on, Sam, we're wanting this investigation over with. Spill whatever you're thinking."

Sam gave Rachel an apologetic look. "There's one thing I had a question about, that's all. I was speaking to somebody who grew up here." She paused, trying to protect Vanessa's identity. "They were saying you and Dom actually knew each other when you were kids. That Dom was something of a bully."

Rachel was still for a few moments. She sighed, looking at the floor. Arlo gave her a sympathetic look, and she reached down to pet him. "That must have been Vanessa." Sam's expression must have given her away, because Rachel said, "Don't worry, I won't tell her you said anything. She's not wrong. Dom and I go way back. He was causing issues for me even in middle school. He made my life miserable—I didn't even want to go to school for years. It was a struggle for my mom to get me there every day."

Nora drew in a sharp breath. "That man! I didn't have any idea."

"It wasn't fun," said Rachel. "But just to be clear—that was a long time ago. People change, or at least they're supposed to when they grow up. Once I graduated, I figured I'd left all that behind. When the restaurant got those nasty reviews from Dom, though, it felt like history repeating itself. He had a knack for making life hard for me."

Nora scowled. "Why would he pick on you at school? And why now? It doesn't make any sense."

"Bullying never makes any sense," said Rachel with a shrug. She paused. "I've always thought the thing that really triggered it was in high school. I reported Dom for cheating on a test. The teacher was one of those old-school types, and he flunked Dom for the entire semester. He was a guy who believed in consequences. That's when Dom's bullying intensified. I think he always hated me after that."

Nora said furiously, "He should have blamed himself for being stupid enough to cheat. If that man weren't already dead, I'd murder him myself."

"Believe me, I had some real grievances with Dom. But I'm no killer. I didn't exactly wish the guy well, but I didn't lay a hand on him or Olivia."

"Thanks for clarifying that, Rachel. I knew you couldn't have anything to do with what happened, but I thought you should know what I heard." Sam waited a moment. "There was just one other thing. You were complimenting the monkey wallpaper in my bathroom. You'd seen it the night of the dinner party."

Nora snorted. "Monkey wallpaper." She cast a haughty glance toward the half-bath.

"I thought it was cute," said Rachel with a grin.

"The only problem is that there's no monkey wallpaper in there." Sam gave her an apologetic look. She really did like Rachel. But she didn't want to give her a pass if she'd killed Dom.

Nora stared at Rachel, looking shocked.

Rachel said slowly, "Gotcha. And you're right . . . I didn't go to the restroom. I went out on the terrace. Like I said, the whole reason I'd crashed your party was to talk to Dom. I mean, I didn't *want* to talk to him since he was in such a bad mood. I kind of thought I might be going on a fool's errand. But I also felt like I didn't have any other choice. So I squared my shoulders and headed outside to do it. I needed a loan if I'm going to reopen the restaurant."

"And you killed him," said Nora flatly.

"No. I didn't. But somebody had. Dom was already dead when I walked outside."

Sam said, "And you didn't tell anybody."

Rachel shook her head. "I was terrified. I figured the cops would be sure I'd done it." She took a deep breath. "I wiped down the doorhandle on the way in and out of the terrace."

"Ohhh," groaned Nora. Precious looked up at Nora with concern in his eyes before falling back asleep.

"I know. I'm ashamed of myself. It was like I was running on instinct. With all my bad luck lately, the last thing I needed was to be arrested for murder. And I didn't do it. It wasn't me."

Rachel absently brushed the dog fur off her pants. "Anyway, I'm sorry. I shouldn't have wiped down the evidence. And I shouldn't have covered up that I knew Dom was dead." She gave a short laugh. "And I shouldn't have crashed your party, Sam. But now, I've got to try to move forward. I should probably head out on that job search. I need to have some income coming in, at least."

Nora followed suit, her joints creaking as she rose. "Yes, I suppose we should be going too. Come on, Precious," she called to the pit bull, who had been contentedly snoozing near Arlo's bed. Precious yawned, stretched, and ambled over, his pink tutu slightly askew. "This one's probably eager to get home for his afternoon snack," Nora added, fondly patting Precious on the head.

Chapter Nineteen

Sam walked them both to the door, Arlo trotting alongside. "It was good to see you both, despite the circumstances."

As she closed the door behind them, Sam leaned against it, letting out a long breath. The afternoon sun slanted through the windows, reminding her of all the yard work she'd left unfinished.

"What do you say we finish up outside, Arlo?" she asked. The dog wagged his tail in response.

For the next couple of hours, Sam threw herself into weeding and pruning, trying to process everything she'd learned. The physical work helped clear her head, and by the time the sun started setting, the yard looked significantly better.

Exhausted but satisfied, Sam headed inside to shower and make a quick dinner. She spent the evening going over her notes from the day, adding details to her suspect list and trying to connect the dots. But the more she thought about it, the more confused she felt.

As she got ready for bed, she decided a good night's sleep might help her see things more clearly. "Early morning walk tomorrow, Arlo," she said, scratching behind his ears. "We both need to clear our heads."

The next morning, Sam woke right as the first rays of sunlight were peeking over the horizon. Arlo was peeking at her over the covers, a hopeful look in his eyes.

Sam got up, pulled on her exercise clothes and heavier layers for the cold, and headed out to take Arlo on a short walk before feeding him.

The crisp November air nipped at Sam's cheeks. She'd bundled up in a cozy fleece jacket, thermal leggings, and sturdy walking shoes, her breath forming in small clouds in the chilly air. Arlo trotted happily beside her, sporting a jaunty red and black plaid sweater that Sam had found online for him.

As they rounded the corner onto Maple Street, Sam heard the rumble of an approaching car. She recognized Alfred's blue sedan and lifted her hand to wave, a smile already forming on her lips. Arlo's tail wagged in anticipation, clearly hoping for one of Alfred's famous ear scratches.

But as the car drew nearer, Sam's smile faltered. Alfred's usually jovial face was set in tired lines, his eyes fixed straight ahead. She could have sworn he glanced her way for a split second, but he didn't slow down or return her wave. The car continued past them without pause, leaving Sam standing on the sidewalk with her hand still half-raised.

"Well, that was odd," Sam murmured to Arlo, who looked up at her with a quizzical tilt of his head. "I guess Alfred's having a rough morning."

As they continued their walk, Sam couldn't shake the nagging feeling that something was off. Alfred had always been so friendly and quick with a smile or a wave. She made a mental note to check in on him later, her Type-A brain already categorizing this unexpected behavior and filing it away for further investigation.

A cold gust of wind managed to get all the way through the layers to her skin. It felt like it was time to get back home.

"Breakfast?" asked Sam.

Arlo thought that was a marvelous idea. He chased his tail in a circle for several moments before they quickly got back to the house.

It was always refreshing to see how excited Arlo was to eat his meals. It was always the same kibble because Sam was afraid to change the regimen in case it upset what seemed to be his sensitive tummy. No matter what, however, he attacked his food with gusto. Sam opened the fridge and couldn't summon any enthusiasm for its contents. She decided maybe she needed to go to the actual gym to exercise today.

Sam loved working out at home. She had a good deal of equipment downstairs. And it meant she didn't have to commute to a gym—she could just start working out right after she woke up. But she still kept her gym membership for days like these. They had equipment she *didn't* have, and she suspected that she sometimes kept doing the same exercises at home where she should probably work out different muscles. And, perhaps, work up an actual appetite, which she certainly didn't have now.

On the way in, she called Jason to get another status update on Olivia.

"She's mostly the same, but the neurologist says there are positive signs," Jason said, sounding tense. "The doctor says he's going to try and take her from the coma later today. He's cautiously optimistic. They have police stationed here to make sure nothing happens to her. An Officer Martinez. He told me they weren't taking any chances with Olivia's safety. Of course," he added grimly, "Any killer would have to make it past me, first."

Jason quickly got off the phone when the nurse came into the hospital room.

Sam walked into the gym, the familiar scent of disinfectant and sweat mingling in the air. The expansive space was dotted with various machines and free weights, the low hum of treadmills and ellipticals providing a constant background noise. Despite the early hour, there was already a decent crowd of fitness enthusiasts scattered throughout the facility.

She made her way past the row of cardio machines, her eyes scanning the weightlifting area. Sam had a comprehensive set of dumbbells at home, but the gym's array of specialized resistance machines always intrigued her. Today, she was drawn to the cable machine in the corner, perfect for working those stabilizing muscles she often neglected in her home workouts.

As Sam approached the machine, she caught sight of Vanessa Martin across the room. Vanessa was perched on a recumbent bike, her legs moving in a steady rhythm. She wore a mismatched outfit of faded black leggings that had clearly seen better days, paired with a slightly oversized t-shirt that Sam suspected might belong to her husband, Derek. Her hair was pulled back in a messy ponytail, and she seemed to be more focused on people-watching than on her workout.

When Vanessa's eyes met Sam's, there was a flash of recognition followed by something else. Almost a look of urgency. She quickly dismounted the bike and made her way over to Sam, her worn sneakers squeaking slightly on the polished floor.

"Sam!" Vanessa called out, slightly out of breath. "I'm so glad I ran into you here. I was hoping we could talk."

Sam paused, her hand still on the cable machine. She could tell from Vanessa's expression that this wouldn't be a casual gym chat. "Of course," she replied, trying to keep her tone light. "What's on your mind?"

Vanessa glanced around, as if checking for eavesdroppers, before leaning in closer. "It's about Olivia," she said in a low voice. "I heard you were there when they found her. I was hoping you could tell me more about what happened."

Sam felt a twinge of unease. She hadn't expected to be discussing Olivia's attack in between sets at the gym. But as she looked at Vanessa's earnest face, she realized that this conversation was probably inevitable. She nodded and gestured toward a quieter corner of the gym.

"Let's sit down," Sam suggested. They both settled on a bench.

Vanessa looked like she hadn't slept well the night before. "Are you doing all right?" asked Sam.

Vanessa shook her head. "I'm not doing great, actually. I'm having a tough time falling asleep, and when I *do* fall asleep, I'm having these awful nightmares."

"Good for you for going to the gym anyway," said Sam. "I'd think the temptation would be to sleep in."

"I couldn't sleep in even if I wanted to. Derek is up so early to teach, you know. I've always been a pretty light sleeper, and there's no way I can sleep through the sound of the shower running and him getting dressed and making his breakfast." She paused. "Also, I don't think he's crazy about me sleeping in when he has to get up." She shrugged. "So I decided to drag myself to the gym."

Vanessa gave Sam a piercing look suddenly. "I wanted to ask you what you knew about Olivia. Like I said, I heard you're the one who found her."

"Well, myself and her poor brother."

Vanessa nodded. "How's Jason doing?"

"He's worried sick."

Vanessa said, "That's awful. The poor guy." She paused. "What are the cops thinking? Did you talk to them?"

"I'm sure we're all going to be talking to them again. That's protocol, isn't it? I didn't get any useful information from them, though. I was mostly explaining to the police why Jason and I were on the trail and what we saw."

Vanessa looked disappointed. "That's too bad. I was hoping they'd be on the trail of somebody and the rest of us could be let off the hook."

"Do you have an alibi for Olivia's attack? That would probably take you off the suspect list altogether."

Vanessa sighed. "Nope. I was at home, getting caught up on paperwork for my job. Bookkeeping is one of those never-ending chores." She leaned forward. "There's something I think the police should know. I wasn't going to mention it, but Olivia's attack changes things. She was having an affair. Cheating on Dom."

Sam wondered if she was talking about the affair that had happened a while back. The one the police and probably everyone else knew about now.

Vanessa must have been able to read her mind because she said impatiently, "Not that one. A new one. Some man she met in town, I guess. I saw them together downtown a couple of weeks ago. They looked close."

"And you're thinking he might have tried to kill her?" asked Sam slowly.

"Why not? Maybe Olivia wanted to end the affair. She might have felt guilty about it after Dom's death. Maybe the guy didn't want it to be over and lost it." Vanessa shrugged. "Anyway, Olivia's attack could have been totally unrelated to Dom's. I think the police should know about it."

"They probably should." Although Sam wondered if Vanessa had been imagining things. Maybe Olivia and the man were just friends.

Vanessa said, "Believe me, I can't blame her for the affair. I know Dom had a very negative influence on Olivia's life. It would have been challenging for her in that marriage." She made a face. "Besides, I'm not exactly someone who can be judgmental about somebody cheating on their husband, considering I was seeing Dom. I think the reason I haven't been able to sleep is that I'm feeling really guilty about my affair, especially now with Olivia in the hospital."

"Guilty because of Olivia?" To Sam, it felt like Vanessa should feel more guilty about her husband Derek.

Once again, Vanessa seemed to read her mind. "Yeah, I know. I should be feeling bad about letting Derek down. I'm so emotionally messed up right now that I feel like I don't know what I'm thinking. But yes, I do worry about the state of my marriage. Now Dom is gone, and I'm out of the affair. But now I'm taking a long, hard look at my relationship with Derek. Are we even that compatible? It feels like we don't even have the same interests anymore."

"Did you, at one point?"

Vanessa said, "I think so. We'd do things together, at any rate. I mean, we never had two cents to rub together, so they were always cheap things. We'd go to the park and have a picnic, or take a hike. Sometimes we'd hang out in our backyard with a bottle of wine. We don't do anything like that anymore. I feel like Derek and I are practically strangers sometimes."

Sam wasn't sure exactly what to say to this. She wasn't coming from a position of expertise when it came to giving marriage advice. Her own ex-husband was in prison for planning to kill her. Fortunately, Vanessa didn't seem to want advice, just an ear.

"I don't even see a future with the two of us in it. But I've been avoiding confronting Derek about our relationship issues, so there's never any resolution to the problems. Maybe the affair with Dom was my way of avoiding working on my marriage." She shook her head. "Plus, I'm starting to feel a little bored or burned out with the interior design stuff. It often seems like every job is the same. The homeowners always seem to want the same look. It's not as creative as I wanted the job to be."

Sam said, "So you're thinking about getting a fresh start? With maybe a divorce and a new job?"

Vanessa grimaced. "When you put it that way, it seems totally overwhelming to me. I can't even bring myself to sit down with Derek and have a heart-to-heart with him." She sighed. "Anyway, is it really the best time to set out on my own? Derek and I are both suspects in a couple of murders."

"Can you think of somebody else who might have wanted to hurt Dom and Olivia?" asked Sam.

"Well, everybody wanted to hurt Dom. I can't imagine anyone hurting Olivia. Maybe it was one of those things where she knew too much." Vanessa was quiet for a few moments. "I know I thought it was Rachel when I talked to you last time. But I'm having a tough time imagining Rachel shoving Olivia off a cliff."

Which wasn't exactly what happened, but then Vanessa wasn't there. Sam didn't correct her.

Vanessa continued, "I keep thinking about how passionate Rachel is about her family business, though. Maybe Rachel did kill Dom, looking for revenge for him getting her restaurant closed down. If Olivia knew something, it might have put Rachel in the position of thinking she'd have to get rid of Olivia to stay out of prison." She looked curious. "You seem to be talking to people. Is anyone saying that *I* might have done it?"

Jason had, of course. He'd known about Vanessa's affair with Dom because of a one-sided phone argument and then an in-person argument.

Sam said, "I don't think that's something people are saying. But I did pick up that your affair with Dom might not have been as much of a secret as you thought."

Vanessa narrowed her eyes. "That sounds like something Olivia's brother would say."

"What do you mean?"

Vanessa gave a short laugh. "I *thought* I saw Jason that day Dom and I were squabbling out in public. It was a stupid thing to do, but we were alone. But when I turned in his direction, Jason was already gone. I figured maybe I'd imagined him there. Is he throwing me under the bus? Maybe *he's* the one who killed Dom and hurt Olivia, and he's trying to divert attention from himself. After all, if she dies, he gets all that money, which is a huge motive. I bet the cops think so, too."

Sam said, "I didn't say it was Jason."

"You didn't have to. Look, I should get going if I'm going to work out before a client meeting I have. See you later."

Chapter Twenty

S am made it through the workout, although she felt less fo-cused than usual. Her mind kept drifting back to Dom and Olivia and what might have happened to them. Still, she got her exercising done and the appetite she'd been looking for.

The rest of the morning and early part of the afternoon, she worked on housework, then looked at a resident's architectur-al review request for the HOA. After that, she worked on the HOA newsletter, listing the upcoming events.

Following that, she smiled with anticipation. She'd told one of the moms in the neighborhood that her specialty was creating itineraries for vacations. Not that Sam herself had gone on a va-cation lately, but she loved creating them for others. This one was for Disney World, and she'd nearly finished it. After another thirty minutes online, she called the mom up.

"Megan? Hi there, it's Sam. Are you getting excited about your trip to Disney?"

"Hi, Sam! Oh my gosh, the kids are about to drive me nuts, they're so excited."

"I finished up that itinerary for you. Just wanted you to know I've emailed it so you can get it."

"One second," said Megan. "I'll pull it up."

It ended up being somewhat more than a second. Megan apparently not only pulled it up, but was examining the document. "Wow. I mean . . . wow, Sam. You are incredible."

"It was my pleasure! Believe me, this is how I work out stress."

Megan said slowly, "Okay. I don't understand how creating a color-coded spreadsheet to map out someone else's vacation could make you *less* stressed out. But this . . . this is amazing."

"It's got the best times to ride specific attractions to minimize wait times. I also listed optimal routes through the park to reduce walking, and a schedule for character meet-and-greets. There's a tab for food recommendations, too, which I thought might be useful for the kids. It has the best times and places to get specific treats like Dole Whips and Mickey-shaped pretzels."

"Wow," said Megan again, sounding rather overwhelmed.

"Don't forget to download the park app. I've noted the best times to check for FastPass availability."

Megan said, "I just don't know what to say. Thank you! You've made this much easier for me."

Suddenly another call was trying to come in. "Sorry, Megan, I've got to run. I've got another incoming call. Enjoy your trip!"

It was Ginny from the agility club. "Hey there! Am I catching you at a bad time?"

"Not at all. How's it going?"

Ginny said, "Great!"

Sam had the feeling that Ginny's answer would always be the same, no matter when you asked her.

Ginny continued, "Say, we're having another agility night tonight. I know it hasn't been a week yet, but Pixie has way, way too much energy. I called the gang up, and most everybody can make it after five today. Want to join up?"

"Sure, that would be great." Sam looked over at Arlo, who was currently not appearing particularly agile in any way. The little dog yawned. "He's about to sack out for a nap now, but I'm sure I can get him excited about going later on."

"Let him get his rest. He'll be needing it when we meet up later."

Sam smiled as they hung up. After spending a good deal of time at home after Chad was arrested, it was great to feel like she was part of the world again. But, like Arlo, she was feeling sleepy. And she knew herself—if she didn't get some caffeine and a little outside stimulation, it was going to be hard for her to gear up for the agility club.

So instead of making a pot of coffee in her house, Sam decided to head out to the local coffeehouse in Sunset Ridge's cute downtown. She eventually found a parking place in one of the angled spots lining Main Street. School had let out, and the area was bustling with moms and dads taking kids to after-school activities.

She pushed open the heavy wooden door to Bean There, Done That and a burst of warm air carrying the rich aroma of freshly ground coffee enveloped her. The interior of the coffee shop was a blend of modern and rustic elements—exposed brick walls adorned with local artwork, reclaimed wood tables paired with sleek metal chairs, and Edison bulbs casting a soft, warm glow throughout the space.

Sam had developed a fondness for their honey lavender latte. Soon, drink in hand, she turned to find a place to sit. It didn't take long for her to spot Derek Martin, hunched over a corner table near the back. He was surrounded by a stack of papers, a red pen poised in his hand as he frowned at the sheet of paper in front of him. His worn messenger bag was slung over the back of his chair.

After a moment of hesitation, Sam walked over to him. It looked like he was knee-deep in grading papers, and she didn't want to interrupt him. But she also didn't want to hang out in the coffeehouse without greeting him. "Hi there," she said in a quiet voice.

Derek glanced up, then smiled at her. Sam noticed the tired lines around his eyes. "Hi, Sam." He moved some papers aside. "Want to join me?"

"Oh, I don't want to disturb you. It looks like you're knocking out some work."

Derek gave her a wry look. "Believe me, I don't mind the interruption. I'm reading some truly uninspired essays. I'd love to take a break from them."

"Okay, thanks. I won't tie you up too long." She smiled at him. "I needed a little caffeine to keep me going this afternoon."

Derek looked serious. "I bet you do. Aiden told me what happened with Olivia. I'm sorry you had to go through that. I wouldn't blame you for losing sleep."

"Yeah, it hasn't been the easiest week for anybody, has it? Especially for Dom and Olivia."

Derek quickly said, "Exactly. I couldn't believe the news when I heard about Olivia. I didn't really know her well, but she seems like a great person." He rubbed his face tiredly. "I can't believe this is happening. I mean, Maple Hills seems like the safest subdivision around. And there's been a murder and a near-fatal attack in the last week."

"Well, one of them was out on the trail, but I know what you mean. It's tough to process. I keep trying to think everything through."

Derek said, "How's that going for you?"

"Not well. How about you? Have you had time to think about everything?"

"Unfortunately, yes. I've been trying to distract myself with schoolwork, but it's still all jumbled in my mind." He paused. "The police spoke with me again."

It seemed to be the concern for everybody who'd been at Sam's dinner party. Instead of trying to allay Derek's obvious worry, she decided to just be an ear. He seemed like he wanted to talk. "Did they?"

Derek took a sip of his coffee, then nodded. "Yep. They wanted to see where I was around the time Olivia was hurt. I didn't have any kind of alibi."

"Vanessa wasn't at home?"

Derek looked down at the table, hiding the expression in his eyes. "She was out—running errands, I think. Vanessa has been spending as much time out of the house as possible lately. Avoiding me."

Sam frowned. "Avoiding *you*? I'd think it might be the other way around." Plus, Vanessa had said she was at the house getting caught up with bookkeeping for her business.

"Because Vanessa was the one having the affair? I know. But that doesn't seem to be the way it's working. I'm not sure if we're ever going to recover from this, you know?" Derek ran a hand through his hair, his expression a mix of frustration and resignation. "The thing is, Sam, I've known about the affair for a while. I just didn't know how to confront it."

Sam's eyebrows rose in surprise. "You knew? But you didn't say anything to Vanessa about it?"

"I thought if I ignored it, maybe it would go away," Derek admitted, his voice low. "Pretty stupid, huh?"

"It's not stupid," Sam said gently. "It's human."

Derek nodded, then looked Sam directly in the eye. "The police asked me about my relationship with Dom both times they talked to me. They seemed to think I might have had a motive."

"Did you?" Sam asked, keeping her tone neutral.

Derek's laugh was humorless. "Other than the fact that he was sleeping with my wife? No, not really. I actually admired Dom quite a bit, aside from when he was acting like a jerk. He might not have looked it, but he was a financial whiz. He had a real gift for finance."

Sam noticed a flicker of something—admiration? resentment?—cross Derek's face.

"The evening Olivia was attacked," Derek continued, his voice dropping even lower, "I was grading papers at home, like I said. But I went for a walk around the neighborhood to clear my head. I didn't see anyone, and no one saw me. Not exactly a solid alibi. And I did leave the house."

"Vanessa was gone the whole time?"

Derek blinked, then said, "Actually, she came home while I was out walking. We passed each other in the driveway." He gave a short laugh. "We barely spoke two words to each other."

There was something off about Derek's tone, but Sam couldn't quite put her finger on it. Was he covering for Vanessa? Or was there more to his story than he was letting on?

"Derek," Sam said carefully, "is there anything else you want to tell me? Anything that might help make sense of all this?"

Derek stared into his coffee cup for a long moment. When he looked up, his eyes were filled with a mix of emotions Sam couldn't quite decipher.

"I wish I knew a way to make sense of it all, Sam. I really wish I knew."

They were quiet for a few moments as they sipped their coffees and listened to the acoustic cover of a popular indie song that was playing in the background.

Sam said slowly, "Last time we talked, you mentioned that you thought Jason Barnes might have been responsible for Dom's death. Do you still feel that way?"

"As far as I can tell, Jason had even more motive to murder Olivia than he did to murder Dom. I gather he'll inherit the entire estate if Olivia doesn't make it. At least, that's what the local gossips are saying."

Sam said, "That's what I've heard, too. But would Jason really murder his own sister? They both said they were very close when they were growing up. And Olivia took Jason in when he had nowhere else to go."

"Greed can do terrible things to people, though. Besides, there was a lot of stress in that house. Can you imagine living day-to-day with Dom? Dom clearly didn't want Jason in the house. It was a tough situation and the cracks were probably starting to show. Maybe Jason snapped."

Sam paused. "Speaking of gossip and rumors, I did have one thing I wanted to ask you."

"Sure, shoot." But Derek tensed up.

"I heard that you and Dom had a blow-up recently. And that you were in close proximity to the door that led out to the terrace."

Now Derek looked angry. In a stiff voice, he said, "Whoever said that is lying. It's those kinds of lies that could make me lose my job. Nobody's going to hire me to work with kids if there's a cloud of suspicion hanging over me. Who said that?"

Sam wasn't about to mention Olivia's name. Instead, she said vaguely, "It was just a rumor."

"Dom annoyed me, don't get me wrong. He was totally trying to bait me at the dinner party, and trying to get under Vanessa's skin, too. But I would never have laid a finger on him."

It seemed like there was really nothing left to say. Sam said, "I know you wouldn't. And I'm sorry I kept you away from your grading for so long." She slid back her chair to stand up.

Derek reached out a hand to stop her. "No, *I'm* sorry. I shouldn't have snapped at you like that. Chalk it up to lack of sleep or stress. Or both. Let's change the subject, okay? There was something I wanted to ask you."

Sam settled back into the chair. "Sure."

Derek gave her a curious look. "If you don't mind me asking, what's going on between you and Aiden?"

"What?" Sam blinked at him, startled. She felt a slight warmth creep into her cheeks. "Aiden and I are just friends," she said, trying to keep her tone casual. "He's been helpful with some of the neighborhood issues, given his background in law enforcement. He's given me some ideas about improving Maple Hills safety and communication."

She paused, considering how much to share. "I appreciate his insights, especially with everything that's been happening lately. But that's all there is to it."

Derek raised an eyebrow, a knowing smile playing at the corners of his mouth. "If you say so. Aiden's a good guy, you know. One of the best teachers we have at the school."

Sam nodded, feeling slightly flustered. "I'm sure he is. Anyway, I should probably get going. Thanks for talking with me, Derek."

As she gathered her things, Sam couldn't help but wonder why Derek's question about Aiden had caught her so off guard. She pushed the thought aside, focusing instead on what she'd learned during their conversation.

Chapter Twenty-One

Back at home, Arlo greeted her happily as she walked in the door. Sam got on the floor to love on him for a few minutes. She'd never had pets when she was growing up because her mother and father didn't want any mess. Sam never knew how much she'd missed out on. Having Arlo be so delighted that she was home warmed her heart.

"Hey, you want to go to agility in a little bit? See your new friends?"

Arlo indicated he did.

"Okay. But then you and I are going to have a super-quiet night, okay? I'm thinking we're going to do a movie night."

Arlo's tail wagged, as if he knew exactly what Sam was saying.

Sam said, "And I know the last movie night didn't go entirely as planned. I ended up getting distracted during the film and organized the kitchen. But that won't happen this time."

Arlo licked her chin in an understanding manner.

Soon, it was time to go. As they arrived, Sam pulled into the makeshift parking area for her second visit to the agility club. She saw dogs of all sizes darting between colorful obstacles, their barks filling the air. Arlo's tail wagged furiously in the backseat.

As they approached the group, Sam spotted Ginny's wild red curls bouncing as she directed Pixie through a series of jumps. Several other club members were scattered across the field, some practicing weave poles, others attempting the seesaw.

"Sam! Arlo!" Ginny called out, waving them over. "Come see what Pixie learned this week."

Sam watched, impressed, as Ginny and Pixie demonstrated a complex weave pole sequence. The tiny Jack Russell terrier zipped in and out of the poles with lightning speed, barely seeming to touch the ground.

"Wow, that's amazing," Sam said, genuinely awed. "I don't know if Arlo and I will ever get to that level."

Dave chuckled, coming up beside her with Rocket, his border collie, at his heels. "Don't worry, you'll get there. Why don't you two try the tunnel? Arlo seemed to enjoy that last time."

Sam nodded, leading Arlo to the large fabric tunnel. With a bit of coaxing and a treat held at the exit, Arlo darted through, emerging with a proud doggy grin on his face.

"Great job, Arlo!" Lucy called from nearby, where she was adjusting Ziggy's harness. The whippet sat patiently, tail sweeping the ground.

As Sam praised Arlo, she noticed a new addition to the group, a young woman with a small, trembling chihuahua in her arms.

Ginny, ever the welcoming committee, bounded over. "Everyone, this is Melissa and Peanut. It's their first time, so let's make them feel at home."

The group gathered around, dogs sniffing curiously at the newcomers. Peanut looked terrified at first, but as Melissa set him down, he cautiously explored, gaining confidence with each step.

"Don't worry, Melissa," Sam said. "Arlo and I were new last week. Everyone here is really helpful."

Melissa smiled gratefully. "Thanks. I'm hoping this might help with Peanut's anxiety. He's a rescue, and he's still pretty nervous around other dogs and people."

Sam nodded understandingly. "Arlo's a rescue too. This has been great for building his confidence."

As if to demonstrate, Arlo chose that moment to trot over to Peanut, gently sniffing the smaller dog and wagging his tail in a friendly manner. Peanut, after a moment's hesitation, gave a tentative wag in return.

"All right, folks!" Ginny called out, clapping her hands. The sharp sound echoed across the fenced training field, causing a few of the dogs to perk up their ears. "Let's set up for some obstacle sequences. Experienced handlers and our second-timers, you know the drill. Melissa and Peanut, why don't you just observe for now, and we'll get you started soon."

The regulars, along with Sam and Arlo, spread out across the field. Some headed toward the weave poles, others to the A-frame or tunnel entrances. Sam felt a surge of confidence as she led Arlo toward the jumps they had practiced last week.

Ginny's eyes twinkled as she addressed Melissa. "Take a moment to observe how the handlers guide their dogs through the course. Pay attention to the hand signals and verbal cues they use. Sam and Arlo can show you some basics in a moment."

Sam wasn't at all sure she could show anybody anything yet. But then she remembered how she'd always cemented information in her head better when she was showing it to someone else. She supposed if she ran into trouble, she could always ask somebody else for help.

As the pairs navigated the obstacles, Ginny walked among them, offering advice and adjusting positions. The field filled with a cacophony of barks, the thump of paws on equipment, and the occasional cheer when a dog completed a particularly challenging sequence.

Sam found herself next to Dave and his border collie again. "Ready for round two?" he asked with a friendly smile.

Sam nodded, feeling more prepared than last week. "Arlo and I have been practicing our turns in the backyard. We're excited to try them out."

Dave chuckled. "That's the spirit. You'll be surprised how quickly you both pick it up."

As they watched, Ginny showed a slightly more complex sequence with Pixie. "Remember, it's all about maintaining that connection with your dog," she called out. "Sam, why don't you show Melissa how you and Arlo tackle the tunnel and jump combination?"

Sam felt a flutter of nerves, but also a spark of excitement. She led Arlo to the start of the sequence, aware of Melissa and Peanut watching intently.

"Ready, Arlo?" she asked, and her furry companion looked up at her with eager eyes. As they began the sequence, Sam felt the thrill of working in tandem with Arlo, their movements becoming more synchronized with each obstacle.

After completing the sequence, Sam turned to Melissa with a grin. "See? It's not so scary once you get started. You and Peanut will be doing this in no time."

Melissa smiled back, looking more relaxed. Peanut, watching from her arms, gave a little tail wag.

"All right," Ginny announced, "let's pair up and work on some more advanced sequences. Sam, why don't you work with Melissa on some basic commands while I set up the next challenge?"

Sam was surprised to find that she'd remembered more than she'd realized. She showed Melissa and Peanut various commands while they listened with interest. Then it was time for a water break for the dogs. While the dogs rested and visited with each other, their owners were doing some visiting of their own. Sam walked around chatting to different people and trying to commit their names and faces to memory.

Toward the end of the break, Dave approached Sam with a thoughtful look on his face. "Hey, Sam, I hope you don't mind me asking, but I overheard you mentioning to Lucy earlier that you were trying to help someone find a job. A friend of yours?"

Sam nodded, careful with her words. "Yes, his name is Jason. He's been going through a tough time lately."

Dave rubbed the back of his neck. "Well, I work at Sunset Ridge Credit Union. We're actually looking for someone in our customer service department. Entry-level position, but with room for growth. If your friend is good with people, it might be worth looking into."

Sam smiled, surprised by this potential opportunity. "That's really kind of you, Dave. I'll definitely pass that information along to Jason. He could use some good news right now."

Dave smiled. "Happy to help. You know, it's funny—we rarely have many openings, but there's been some shuffling around lately."

Sam tried to keep her expression neutral. "Is the banking community here pretty tight-knit? Would you know Dom Stanton?"

Dave nodded, his expression turning serious. "Yeah, he was a high-ranking officer at one of the big banks, of course. Brilliant with finances, but . . ." He trailed off, then lowered his voice. "Look, I probably shouldn't say this, but Dom wasn't the easiest person to deal with. He had a way of making everyone feel inferior, from tellers to fellow executives. I hate to speak ill of the dead, but I can't say I was surprised to hear he'd made some enemies. At least, I guess he did, since somebody murdered him."

Sam nodded thoughtfully, filing away this new information about Dom. "Thanks for sharing that, Dave. And thanks again for the job lead. I'm sure Jason will appreciate it."

"No problem," Dave replied. "Just tell your friend to mention my name if he applies. And Sam?" He paused, looking uncomfortable. "I know there's been a lot of talk around town about what happened. I heard Dom was at your place when it all happened. It sounds like you've been through a lot lately. If you ever need someone to talk to, we're all here for you."

"Thanks, Dave. That means a lot."

They practiced for a while longer, until the wind started really whipping up, blowing a frigid November breeze over them all. Ginny called it a night, and Arlo and Sam set off for home. As promised, Sam found herself curled up on the couch, Arlo nestled comfortably in her lap. The TV was on, playing a light-hearted romantic comedy that Sam had chosen specifically because it required minimal mental engagement. A bowl of "pupcorn" — popcorn popped with grapeseed oil, nutritional yeast, and a sprinkle of dog-safe thyme—sat on the coffee table within easy reach.

"Okay, Arlo," Sam said, scratching behind his ears, "tonight is all about relaxation. No lists, no planning, no thinking about the HOA or anything murder-related." She took a deep breath, trying to will her body to unwind.

Arlo looked up at her with his soulful eyes, his tail thumping gently against the couch cushions. Sam couldn't help but smile. "You're right, buddy. I should take relaxation lessons from you."

As the movie played, Sam found her mind wandering to the to-do list she'd left unfinished on her desk. She caught herself mentally organizing tomorrow's schedule and gave herself a little shake. "Focus on the movie, Sam," she muttered.

Arlo, sensing her tension, nuzzled his head under her chin. Sam laughed softly, the sound surprising her. "Thanks for the reminder, little guy." She reached for the bowl of pupcorn, offering a piece to Arlo before taking one for herself.

As Arlo crunched happily on his treat, Sam found herself actually paying attention to the movie, even chuckling at a particularly witty line.

"You know, Arlo," she said, running her fingers through his soft fur, "I think I'm starting to get the hang of this relaxation thing. Maybe we should make pupcorn night a regular occurrence."

Arlo's enthusiastic tail wag seemed to indicate his wholehearted agreement. As the credits rolled, Sam realized she'd made it through the entire movie without once reaching for her phone or planner. After that personal success, she called it a day.

Chapter Twenty-Two

The following afternoon, there was a knock at her door. Sam opened it to find Mandy standing there. It had started raining, and a wind was kicking up. Mandy didn't seem to have dressed with any thought to the weather.

"Gracious, it's freezing!" said Sam. "Come on inside."

Mandy hesitated. "I might track in or dribble rain on your furniture."

"Don't even think about it. Here, let's turn the fire on." With a click of a remote, Sam had a gas fire roaring. She pointed to one of the two armchairs in front of it. "Please, have a seat. I'll get us something to drink. Water? Or maybe a glass of wine?"

"A glass of wine would be great," said Mandy, sounding as if she needed it.

Sam returned a few minutes later with a tray holding two glasses of Pinot Noir and a dish with roasted pecans. Arlo had cuddled up with Mandy in the chair.

"Should I get him to jump down?" asked Sam.

"No, he's making me feel better," said Mandy with a short laugh. "Arlo's a good boy."

Arlo gave Mandy a loving look and snuggled even more.

"Is everything all right?" asked Sam. She suddenly felt very guilty that she hadn't checked on Mandy lately.

Mandy shook her head. "Not really, Sam. I'm so worried about Alfred. I took this afternoon off from work because I couldn't even focus." She took a cautious sip of the wine, then a big gulp.

Sam thought about how she'd seen Alfred on his way to work the other day. How he'd seemed to see her walking Arlo, but then acted as if he hadn't.

"What's happened to Alfred?"

Mandy blew out a breath. "I don't know. He's not acting like himself at all, Sam. Ever since your dinner party, he hasn't been the same. I kept asking him what was going on, but he'd cut me off, saying everything was fine. But I knew it wasn't."

Sam nodded. "I saw him driving on his way to work the other day. He looked pretty grim, especially for Alfred. He's always such an upbeat guy."

"Exactly," said Mandy quickly. "So I started snooping around this afternoon while he was at work. I didn't know what else to do. I went through his laptop and looked at his emails. I really feel ashamed of myself."

"It sounds like you were just trying to understand the best way to help him. Especially since he wasn't being open with you."

Mandy looked relieved. "I'm glad you think so. I've always totally trusted Alfred. And I know he'd never be unfaithful or anything like that. My worry was that his mood started when Dom died."

They were quiet for a few moments, drinking the wine and looking into the fire. Then Sam said, "Did you find anything while you were searching?"

"I did. I saw a note Dom Stanton had handwritten in a pile of Alfred's stuff. It had an amount of money on it—a sizeable amount of money. And some terms? It looked like a loan."

Sam felt a little uncomfortable being ahead of Mandy on the loan. "Like a bank loan?"

"No. No, it was more like a loan Dom made directly to Alfred." Mandy sounded so miserable that Arlo lifted his head to give her a sorrowful look before snuggling his head under her chin in solidarity with her pain. She gave a little sob and buried her face in his fur.

Sam got up to find some tissues. When she came back with the box, Mandy took them from her, but looked a lot more composed. "I'm sorry, Sam. It's not like you don't have anything going on. I don't know what to do. I can't believe Alfred would ever hurt anybody, even Dom. Although Dom was taunting him at the party, wasn't he?"

"Dom was being unpleasant to just about everybody," said Sam. She gave Mandy a crooked smile. "Nora was the only one to escape unscathed."

"That's because he was probably terrified of Nora, the way we all are," said Mandy with a laugh. Then her expression became sad again. "Anyway, I know Alfred is innocent. But why would he borrow money from Dom?"

Sam said carefully, "Are you having . . . I mean, are the two of you having any financial issues?"

"Of course we are! But we always do. We live life on a shoestring budget, and that hasn't changed a bit. So why now? Why would Alfred think we needed money now? And go to *Dom*? He was the kind of guy who'd hold that over our heads. Maybe Alfred couldn't pay back the money when he was supposed to." She leaned her head back on the backrest of the armchair. "I don't know what to think."

"Shouldn't you ask Alfred about it?"

Mandy looked alarmed. "No, that's exactly what I don't want to do. Then he'll know I've been snooping around. That I didn't trust him."

"Just tell him what you told me. That you were concerned about him, about his change of mood. That you care about him. Although I'm sure Alfred knows that. It's so obvious that the two of you love each other."

This statement had the unintended consequence of making Mandy burst into tears again. She grabbed a couple of tissues from the box and said, "Sorry, sorry. You're right, Sam. I need to talk with Alfred. With a marriage like ours, there shouldn't be any secrets."

Sam's response was cut short by a tremendous peal of thunder, then a downpour. Sam frowned. "A thunderstorm? In November?"

Mandy gave a short laugh. "Lately, I'd believe anything is possible."

Then Mandy's phone rang. She glanced at it and froze. "It's Alfred. Shoot. I wanted to figure out what to say to him before I talked to him."

Sam glanced at her watch. "He's probably just come home from work and is wondering where you are. You walked here, right?"

Mandy nodded. Then she picked up the phone. "Hi, love. Yes, I'm fine—I'm here at Sam's house. I walked here before the storm started." She listened for a few moments, gently stroking Arlo and gazing into the fireplace as the flames flickered around the gas logs. "Okay. Yes." She hung up. "Alfred's coming over to pick me up. Says he'll visit for a few minutes first." She gave Sam a grimacing smile. "Will it be awful of me to stick you in the middle of this? I don't want to screw things up with Alfred. But I don't think I can get a minute's rest if I don't talk this out with him right now."

"Of course you want to get it over with. And I'm happy to be here with you if you need support while you bring everything up."

Mandy reached out to squeeze Sam's hand. A minute later, Alfred was at the door, giving a light knock. Arlo hurried over to greet the big man. Sam could still see the tense lines around Alfred's eyes that showed he was still going through whatever inner turmoil he'd been suffering lately. But he reached down to pick up Arlo and love on the little dog for a minute, burying his bearded face in his fur.

Sam smoothly went into hostess mode again. "Come join us by the fire, Alfred." She pulled over another chair before Alfred could step in to help. "Mandy and I are having a glass of wine. Would you like a glass, too?"

"Naw, I'm okay, but thank you, Sam."

They settled in front of the fire, Arlo happily moving over to Alfred's broad lap. Alfred turned his head to look at his wife and saw the box of tissues and the crumpled evidence in Mandy's hand. "Honey," he said in alarm. "What happened?"

Mandy gave Sam a miserable look, as if she really didn't want to launch into the conversation. After waiting a few moments, Alfred turned to look at Sam. "Sam? What's going on?"

Sam cleared her throat. "Actually, that's what Mandy wanted to ask you, Alfred. She's been very worried about you over the last week." Sam waited for Mandy to take up where she'd left off.

Mandy took a deep breath. "Like Sam said, you've got me worried, Alfred. You've been so different lately. Moody. Wanting to be by yourself. And you wouldn't talk with me about it."

Alfred looked taken aback. "I didn't want to trouble you, Mandy. Sometimes folks have problems, you know. This is just one of those times. It's something I've got to work out on my own, that's all."

Mandy was shaking her head. "No, that's exactly what you *shouldn't* do, Alfred. No secrets, right? What's the purpose of a marriage if you can't share your problems with your husband or wife?" She paused. "Besides, I think I know part of it, anyway. You borrowed money from Dom, didn't you?"

Sam was feeling very much like she should leave them to a private conversation. But Mandy gave her a pleading look.

"How did you know about that?" Alfred sounded tired, not angry.

"Oh, honey. I looked through your stuff. I'm sorry. I was so concerned. I saw what looked like an I.O.U."

Alfred rubbed Arlo for a few moments, saying nothing. Then he said in a low voice, "I should never have borrowed money from that man. I don't know what I was thinking. But I was in tough place, and I didn't know what to do."

"What kind of tough place?" Mandy looked anxious. She took a gulp of wine from her glass, as if numbing herself in advance to whatever Alfred was about to say.

Alfred sighed. "You know we've never had much money. I needed some for something. I went to Dom's office at the bank. But he said I wasn't a fit candidate for a bank loan. Then he said he could personally spot me some money. That's when the whole thing became a nightmare."

"Money for what?" pressed Mandy. "I thought we were doing okay. I mean, we didn't have enough for vacations, but we were paying our bills just fine."

Alfred shook his head. "It's a health thing. Nothing to worry about. I've got it all under control."

"What? What kind of health thing?"

Alfred sighed. "I went to the doctor because I was having trouble with pain. I thought maybe I'd pulled something at work or when I was sleeping."

"You didn't tell me about it?" Mandy's voice was hurt.

"I didn't want to worry you. The doctor said it was a degenerative spinal condition."

Mandy sat there, eyes wide.

"I thought I could handle it on my own. It's the kind of thing that causes chronic pain and limits my movement. Or range of movement. Something like that. Anyway, the medical bills were coming to my phone so you wouldn't know about it all. The problem was that I've had to see specialists and physical therapists. The bills were piling up."

"Oh, Alfred."

"It's like the deeper I got into this mess, the harder it was to tell you anything about it." Alfred looked defeated. "I was lying about going to work instead of to the doctor, about the bills, about borrowing from Dom. And then I was tired out all the time, and that made it tough to put on a brave face and act normal. It got even worse when Dom started giving me a hard time."

Mandy said, "A hard time? What did Dom do?"

Alfred rubbed his face. "Well, he changed the interest rates on me, first. Keep in mind, this was a private loan, not a bank loan."

"An interest rate on a private loan?" asked Mandy.

"Well, sure. Dom wasn't going to lend money to me out of the kindness of his heart. He wanted something out of it. He and I weren't friends. Anyway, at first, the interest rate was reasonable. But then, after I took the money, Dom started changing the terms so I was owing more and more. I couldn't keep up."

Sam frowned. This sounded like exactly what she would expect of Dom. But if you were in a real financial spot, how many options did you actually have?

Alfred continued. "Then it got even worse. Dom changed the repayment schedule. He wanted the money paid back quicker than he'd told me at the beginning. When I couldn't do it, Dom started making all these threats. Saying I was going to face real consequences if I didn't give him the money."

"Oh, Alfred," said Mandy again. Her eyes filled with tears.

"Yeah, it was all I could think about. I couldn't even really focus on the treatment I was getting for the medical problem. I was awake at night thinking of ways to make more money. I figured maybe I could make a few extra bucks mowing people's lawns on the weekends. Or maybe working part-time at night. But I knew if I started doing that, you might catch on, Mandy. Wonder why we suddenly needed the extra money."

Mandy said, "Now, look. The only thing important is your health. And our marriage. We can figure this out together."

Alfred shook his head. "It's okay. After Dom died, I visited Olivia in person. She immediately wrote off my debt. I went over there sort of hat-in-hand to ask her if the terms could be changed. But she said she considered the debt paid off." His face darkened. "The cops found out I was at Olivia's place. They've been asking a lot of questions."

Mandy put her hand to her throat. "You need to tell them what happened, Alfred. Lying to the police is going to make things worse than they already are."

"But if I tell them what happened, I'm going to be even more of a suspect than I was before. What do you think, Sam?"

Weighing each word, Sam replied, "I don't really know what you should do. I can see both sides. The problem is that it gives you more of a motive to have killed Dom. But I can't see why you'd have wanted to try to murder Olivia."

"See?" said Mandy. "You've gotta be honest with the police."

"But it's just my word that Olivia erased my debt. It's not like I got anything in writing. As far as the police would know, I attacked Olivia because I couldn't pay back the debt and she wouldn't forgive it."

Mandy groaned, dropping her head in her hands. Arlo, still in Alfred's lap, watched her with concern on his small face.

Alfred gave Sam a pleading look. "You believe me, don't you Sam?"

She did. "Of course I do. And I know it looks bad right now, but there are other people who had motive to kill Dom, too. And Olivia, if she suspected who'd murdered her husband."

"Like who?" asked Alfred.

"Well, there's Rachel, for one. She came over to my dinner party for the express purpose of crashing it, and telling Dom off. He ruined her restaurant business. And it wasn't only a restaurant to Rachel—it was part of her family's heritage."

Alfred and Mandy looked a bit more cheerful at the prospect of someone else with a good motive. "That's true," said Mandy. She blushed. "It does feel bad to be glad somebody else is in trouble."

"It's totally understandable, given the circumstances. Then, of course, we have Jason, Olivia's brother."

Alfred grunted. "Dom was awful to him at your party. Just kept hammering on him the whole time. Wouldn't shut up about Jason being jobless and having to live with him and Olivia."

"Right," said Sam. "And now, if Olivia doesn't pull through, Jason's financial problems are probably a thing of the past."

Mandy looked doubtful. "I have a tough time seeing him killing his sister, though. Those two seem real close."

Alfred said, "But you never really know what you might do when you're desperate. Look at me; I never keep secrets like I've been doing recently. So who knows what Jason might have done if he was worried about money. Who else do we have, Sam?" He chuckled, looking better than he had when he'd first come in. "How about Nora? She was at the party. And, looking at Nora's face, she sure didn't like Dom."

Mandy gave a chiding kick at Alfred. "Now, now. Nora couldn't kill a fly. She's just a sweet old lady."

"Are we talking about the same Nora?" asked Alfred, raising his eyebrows.

"Okay, maybe she's not sweet. But I still can't see her murdering Dom."

Sam said, "Alfred's right that she didn't like Dom. Nora sort of adopted Olivia and Rachel as her own. She definitely has her favorites, and Dom had been responsible for hurting both of them in different ways. I could see Nora giving Dom a shove . . . maybe. But Olivia? I can't imagine Nora hurting Olivia in a million years."

Alfred said, "So Jason and Rachel so far. Who else have we got. Oh, I know. Derek and Vanessa were there at the dinner party." He and Mandy exchanged a telling look.

Sam raised her eyebrows. "Am I missing something? What do you know about them?" She hoped they knew about Vanessa's affair with Dom. She hadn't wanted to bring that up, not feeling like spreading gossip.

Sure enough, Mandy said, "Well, I'm not one to gossip much. But Derek and I saw Dom leaving Vanessa's house when Derek's car wasn't there one night. We found out later by looking online that it was parent-teacher conference night. And Derek is a teacher, so that's where he was."

Alfred quickly added, "We're not saying there was funny business going on, but it seemed kinda weird that Dom would be there at all, especially on a night where Derek was gone."

Sam said, "Yeah, it is kind of weird."

"And if they were having an affair," said Mandy, "then maybe Derek killed Dom because he found out about it."

"Or Vanessa killed Dom because he was going to reveal it. Or maybe one of them wanted to end the affair and the other one didn't," said Alfred.

There was a bolt of lightning that further illuminated the room, followed nearly immediately by thunder which seemed to shake the house. Arlo looked a bit unsettled, although he didn't jump out of Alfred's lap.

Alfred said, "Maybe that's our cue, Mandy. I'll drive us back home. How about if I cook us a couple of burgers on the stovetop? We've got a few hamburger buns left over."

Mandy smiled at him. "That sounds good."

"Here, I'll open up the garage so you don't have to walk in the rain to get to the car," said Sam, rising. Arlo hopped down to follow her.

"Thanks, Sam," said Mandy, reaching out to give Sam a hug. "Seriously, thanks a million. I feel so much better."

"I do, too," said Alfred. He gave Sam a one-armed hug, too. Then he said quietly, "Sorry I didn't stop to say hello when you and Arlo were out walking the other day. My head wasn't in the right place."

"I totally understand," said Sam stoutly. "And I hope things start looking up."

"I'm feeling better about things," said Alfred. And it seemed like a cloud had lifted, at least a little.

Chapter Twenty-Three

The storm continued raging outside, and Arlo kept a wary eye on it through the window, flinching a little when the thunder crashed. Sam gathered him up in her arms and snuggled with him in her bedroom with the white noise sound machine on. She had the terrible feeling that the awful man who'd owned Arlo previously had kept the poor little guy chained up in the front yard during storms. She took a few deep breaths to settle herself down after her blood pressure rose at the thought.

Finally, the storm abated enough for them to leave the bedroom and for Sam to get some supper for herself and Arlo.

Sam took a quick look at the weather on her phone. "We'll take a nice walk tomorrow morning," she promised the little dog. "It's supposed to be nice and clear."

He stopped eating long enough to give her a quick wag of his tail.

It took a while for the weather to clear out of there the next morning. The sun came up, then a shower blew in. But finally, it looked as if the sun might be there to stay. Sam promised Arlo she'd follow up on that walk. First, she gave Jason a quick call. He sounded just as tired, but more upbeat. "The neurologist is saying her brain tissue swelling is good. I feel like they think Olivia might actually pull through."

"Have you left the hospital at all?" asked Sam.

"Nope. I've been showering in the hospital shower. Although I could use a change of clothes. And some real food instead of hospital food."

Sam said, "How about if I switch out with you? Let you go home for a while, get some sleep, food, and fresh clothes?"

Jason hesitated. "Thanks, Sam, but I'd rather stick around."

"Got it. Okay, let me bring you some clothes and food. Do you have a key stashed anywhere?"

He did, under a flowerpot on the front porch. Not the most secure thing, probably, but certainly convenient for Sam. First she wanted to cook something comforting for Jason.

A couple of hours later, Sam cautiously entered the ICU room after logging in and getting permission from Officer Martinez to enter. She held a covered plate for Jason, with the rest of the food in a cooler bag. She also had an overnight bag packed with Jason's things on her shoulder. Olivia looked small in the hospital bed, surrounded by tubes and wires, her face partly obscured by medical equipment. The monitors around her blinked and pulsed. The rhythmic whoosh of the ventilator was oddly hypnotic.

Jason looked like he'd aged a decade. His eyes were bloodshot and his hair disheveled.

"Sam," he croaked, his voice rough. "You don't know how much I appreciate this."

Sam held up the dish. "I brought you some chicken pot pie. Maybe it's not appropriate for this time of day, though."

"I can't even keep up with what time of day it even is. Time doesn't pass in a normal way here."

"How are you holding up?" she asked gently.

Jason let out a bitter laugh. "Better than Olivia is."

"But you said there'd been improvement."

Jason's features softened for a moment. "That's right. Maybe things are moving in the right direction." He gave that short laugh again. "Of course, the main thing I've been wanting is beer."

"I didn't pack any of that," said Sam with an apologetic smile.

Jason waved his hand. "It doesn't matter. Olivia wouldn't want me to drown my sorrows right now."

Sam nodded, her heart aching for him. "No, she wouldn't. But she'd understand why you're struggling."

Jason sank into the hospital recliner, his head in his hands. "I keep thinking about Dom's funeral. Olivia was planning it, you know? But I can't deal with that right now. Or, frankly, ever. I couldn't stand the guy."

"I don't think anybody will expect you to follow through with the service," Sam said quickly. "No one would expect you to. And we should expect that Olivia is pulling through and can come up with her own plans."

Jason nodded absently. "Listen," Jason said suddenly, his tone serious. "Like I mentioned, I know I've been drinking. Too much. But I'm going to stop. Olivia always worried about me falling into that trap, like our dad. And like Dom at the end. I owe it to her to do better."

Sam reached out and squeezed his hand. "That's really brave, Jason. Olivia would be so proud."

Sam asked Jason to let her know if there was anything else he needed. "I put a phone charger in your bag, since I know you wouldn't have brought one. Oh, and on a completely different subject— don't pin all your hopes on this, but I spoke to a man who works at the credit union. They could use some help over there. You mentioned you had a business degree, so you might make a good fit." She pulled out her phone and texted Dave's contact information to Jason. "I hope it works out."

"Thanks, Sam," said Jason, looking away as he blinked hard. "I'll get in touch with him now."

After leaving the hospital and driving home, Sam walked in the door to see Arlo looking expectantly at her. Sam and Arlo left the house for as long of a walk as Arlo wanted. It was chilly again outside, but at least it was sunny.

A rainbow made Sam stop, close to her property line. It was beautiful, arching up across the sky. As she looked, she spotted her rather elusive next-door neighbor on his deck. She'd only met Claude a few times, as he enjoyed keeping to his house and didn't show up for neighborhood events. He was an older man with a neatly trimmed goatee, glasses, and—today—a set of binoculars.

Claude stood when he saw Sam, giving her a wave. Sam was a bit surprised by his friendliness, but glad to see it. "Hi, Claude," she called out.

Claude carefully made his way down the stairs leading from his deck to his yard, clearly intent on coming over to speak with her. Arlo watched with interest as the white-haired man approached them.

"Who's this little fella?" asked Claude with a smile.

"This is Arlo. Want to say hi to Claude, Arlo?"

Arlo decided he might actually require a tummy rub from Claude. Claude was kind enough to stoop over and oblige. Sam worried a little over the awkward angle Claude was bending himself into and was ready to grab him in case he started a freefall to the ground.

Fortunately, no fall was forthcoming. Claude managed to get back to a completely upright position with no issues. He said, "I wanted to talk to you about something, Sam."

"Of course. What can I help you with?"

Claude was still gripping his binoculars and was now using them to gesticulate. "It's about your party. The one that Friday night."

"Oh, goodness. I should have run by to apologize to you for all that. I'm afraid it was very loud when the police cars and the ambulances showed up. And the investigators and the forensics team were out there talking very late. Did we wake you up?"

Claude looked rather offended at the thought he might have been asleep. "Certainly not. I was out on my deck, as a matter of fact. Concerned about what was going on. I thought something might have happened to you."

"Oh, I see. I'm sorry I worried you, then."

Claude shook his head, his eyebrows drawing together in a dismissive way. He seemed to want Sam to stop apologizing so he could say what he wanted to say. "Look, the point is, I was out on my deck. With my binoculars."

"Prior to the murder? Or after it?"

"Both," said Claude crisply. "At first to see what was going on over there. It was a little out of the ordinary for you to have a party."

Sam made a mental note to invite Claude the next time she risked having a dinner party. "I see."

Claude continued, "Then, afterward, I tried to see what the police were up to. But I wanted to tell you what I told the cops. Those dolts acted like they thought what I was saying wasn't important."

"Did you see something?" Sam held her breath.

Claude bobbed his head. "I did. I'd been birdwatching, of course."

Sam nodded, although she wasn't sure what birds Claude would have been able to see in the dark, binoculars or not.

"I saw a woman with black hair out there on your terrace. Must have been around the time of the murder because I'd only seen Dom out there before that. It was too cold that night to be outside comfortably."

Sam decided not to inquire if Claude himself had been too chilly outside. There was something else, though. She cleared her throat. "The only problem is that none of the women attending the party had black hair." She said this in a rather apologetic voice.

Claude's expressive eyebrows drew together again. "That's what those cops said."

"We had two blondes, two brunettes, and one white-haired lady," offered Sam helpfully.

"Brunette, then," barked Claude.

"But their hair is more of a light brown. Dirty blonde, maybe. Not dark brown and definitely not black."

Claude said, "The woman's hair was black as coal! It was black, I tell you."

"Okay," said Sam in what she hoped was a soothing voice. "Okay. I got it. I'll keep that in mind. Thanks for letting me know, Claude."

Claude, still looking prickly and not at all appeased, stomped back up to his deck. Arlo and Sam continued on their way. Sam could see why the police were dubious about Claude's claims. Was he just wanting to be part of the excitement? Or had he seen something and misunderstood what he'd seen? Her neighbor did seem to have a lot of time on his hands.

Chapter Twenty-Four

The wind kicked up suddenly, sending a chill through the air. "You okay, there, Arlo?"

Arlo grinned at her, although he picked up his pace. He was wearing a plaid coat that seemed much warmer than his natural coat. He seemed to glance around to see if there was someone he could visit with, since the visit with Claude had been perhaps less than satisfactory. But the streets were deserted, perhaps a result of the chilly weather.

They passed by Nora's house. Part of Sam wanted to see what Nora was up to, and part of her didn't particularly want the trouble. Arlo, however, looked eagerly toward Nora's house. He was quite fond of the old woman and Precious, too.

Nora's door flung open and Nora hollered, "If you hold on a blessed minute, I'll join you. It takes a minute to put a coat on, you know."

"Good morning, Nora. Sure, we'll wait for you."

Arlo looked delighted at the development, although Sam was still weighing whether she was ready for a Nora encounter or not. It didn't really matter whether or not she was, because a few minutes later, Nora and Precious were upon them.

Precious wasn't wearing his tutu, but what looked like a squall jacket lined with fleece. Although Precious was picking at it with his teeth from time to time while Nora scolded him for not being kind to his clothing.

Nora looked at Sam through narrowed eyes. "You haven't found more bodies or horribly injured people, have you?"

"No, not today," said Sam brightly. "I promise that's not my new hobby. I'd just as well not discover more of them at all."

"Hmph," said Nora in a doubtful tone. "All right, then. Well, I saw you coming down the street by yourself, and I really don't think that's safe. Not after what happened to Olivia. We should all be using the buddy system."

"Should we?"

"Absolutely," said Nora, her tone brooking no disagreement. "Everyone who was at your dinner party needs to be watching their back. It's frightful what's happening. It occurred to me in the middle of the night last night that someone could be picking off your guests one-by-one."

This notion of Nora's startled Sam into momentary silence.

Nora warmed to her topic. "Yes, don't you see? It's like one of those Agatha Christie books, isn't it? The murderer starts killing each of the guests."

"*And Then There Were None*?" Sam didn't think the scenario was remotely like the book. For one thing, they were in the mountains, not on a remote island. And it wasn't a house party. Actually, there were no similarities at all that Sam could see.

"Precisely!" said Nora. "So don't walk Arlo on your own until this case is wrapped up. I called the police today."

"Already?"

Nora sniffed. "Naturally. They're a twenty-four-hour establishment, you know. I told them it was unforgiveable for them not to have arrested the perpetrator. The perp."

"You seem to know your criminal justice lingo."

Nora said, "I like watching *Law and Order* reruns. Anyway, I gave the cops a piece of my mind. Maybe that's what it takes to get results. Citizens have to be pushy and make them realize when something is a priority."

Sam suspected the police ordinarily prioritized murder, especially when two of them had been committed in the same vicinity. But she nodded, wanting to stay on Nora's good side.

"Smoking!" snarled Nora.

Sam started guiltily, although she'd never smoked a day in her life. "Smoking? No, I've never smoked."

"Not you. That Vanessa. I can't believe we have a smoker in the neighborhood." Nora gestured to Vanessa, bundled up in a black coat and matching beret, who was on the phone smoking outside of her house.

Sam had the feeling Vanessa likely wasn't the only smoker in the neighborhood. After all, Dom had stepped out onto her terrace for his fateful cigarette break. However, she certainly wasn't going to broach this with Nora. "Maybe she's trying to quit," said Sam mildly. "I understand it's a hard habit to break."

Nora's face was thunderous. "And she's standing on her own. The neighborhood is too quiet for Vanessa to be by herself. We should stand with her."

Sam said uneasily, "She's probably on a business call, Nora. Remember, she's an interior designer. She may not want two women and two dogs suddenly in her yard while she's trying to concentrate."

But her words fell on deaf ears. Nora was already stomping her way over to Vanessa, Precious in tow. Reluctantly, Sam followed her. She could only imagine Nora's fury if she and Arlo continued on without Nora and Precious as escorts.

Vanessa looked quite surprised as they hovered nearby. She hastily stubbed out her cigarette after Nora violently swatted at the air in front of her face, as if battling an invisible swarm of bees.

"Yes, I'll be there in an hour. I'm sure I'll be able to come up with a plan to make your home office the way you want it. Yes. Thank you." Vanessa hung up the phone, looking at Nora and Sam with mild impatience but also a bit of curiosity. "Is something wrong?"

"Something is most definitely wrong," said Nora. "I just finished explaining to Sam why none of us can be by ourselves outside. The buddy system is absolutely vital right now."

Vanessa looked up at Sam, seeming to seek an explanation which might make more sense than what Nora was saying. Sam shrugged apologetically in response.

"Are you saying that because of the murders in the neighborhood?" Vanessa lifted a blonde eyebrow.

"Of course I am," said Nora. "Can't you see why? Someone is eliminating the dinner party guests. You shouldn't be outside by yourself."

"Shouldn't I?"

"No," said Nora flatly. "And you shouldn't be smoking those cancer sticks."

Vanessa colored a little. "Well, I'm trying to stop."

"You're not doing good job at stopping. Cigarettes wouldn't be in your mouth if you'd stopped." Nora's own mouth pulled downward in dissatisfaction. "Think about your beautiful coat and hat. They're going to be full of nasty cigarette smoke. It will turn them yellow."

Sam wasn't entirely sure a black beret and coat would turn yellow from cigarette smoke. But she certainly wasn't going to weigh in on it.

Nora continued, "And if your outerwear turns yellow, just think what your internal organs must look like. Revolting!"

Vanessa was starting to look very tired.

Sam tried to steer the conversation away from smoking. "Well, your coat and beret are gorgeous. Didn't you wear them to the dinner party?"

"Yes, I did. You have a good eye for detail, Sam. You'll remember, I stepped outside to make that business call. It was so windy that I bundled up."

"Gloves too, I'd imagine."

Vanessa stiffened almost imperceptibly. "Yes, of course. Talking on a phone is hard when your fingers are frozen."

"Well, it's a good thing you don't have them on now," said Nora tartly. "I can't imagine trying to get smoke out of gloves."

"Yes," said Vanessa. "Anyway, I should be getting along. I've got a client meeting to prepare for." She gave them both a tight smile and hurried back into her house.

Nora and Sam moved back out to the sidewalk. "I'm not sure I like that young woman very much," said Nora. "She seems kind of hard."

Sam was sure she and Nora had likely contributed to Vanessa's hardness during their conversation. "Vanessa was busy, and we ambushed her."

"We saved her from herself," said Nora with a sniff. "She should be grateful."

As they continued on their walk, Nora launched into a monologue on various grievances she had with different residents along the way, gesturing wildly with her free hand while Precious trotted along obediently.

"And don't get me started on the Johnsons at number 42," Nora huffed. "They've got the audacity to park their RV in the driveway. It's an eyesore! I've reported it to the HOA three times already."

Sam nodded politely, trying to keep up with Nora's rapid-fire complaints.

"Oh, and the Petersons? They've got a bird feeder that's attracting squirrels. Squirrels! Do you know what those little rats with fluffy tails did to my begonias last year?"

Before Sam could answer, Nora barreled on. "And Mrs. Fitzgerald's wind chimes. I could go on for days about that. It's like living next to a Buddhist monastery. I haven't had a moment's peace since she put those infernal things up."

Arlo's ears perked up as they passed a house with a neatly manicured lawn.

"Ah, the Thompsons," Nora said with a sneer. "Did you know they use a lawn service? Lazy, if you ask me. I swear they're cutting their grass a quarter-inch shorter than regulation. I've got half a mind to get out there with a ruler."

Sam stifled a laugh, picturing Nora army-crawling across the Thompsons' lawn with a tape measure.

"Oh, and that new family on Maple Street? They've got a teenager who insists on practicing his electric guitar with the garage door open. It's like living next to a cut-rate rock concert. I've started timing his sessions. Would you believe he played 'Smoke on the Water' for 87 minutes straight yesterday?"

As they rounded a corner, Nora's eyes narrowed at a house with a small vegetable garden in the front yard. "The Carters think they're so clever with their 'urban farming.' Mark my words, Sam, one day we'll wake up to find chickens roaming the streets. Chickens!"

Nora clearly felt a passionate disdain for her neighbors' harmless activities. It was clear that in Nora's mind, she was the last bastion of civility in a neighborhood teetering on the brink of chaos.

Finally, they reached Sam's house again. Nora gave her a grim look. "No more solo walks until this is all over. Call me. I've got an errand to run later, but then I'll be back home."

Sam said, "But what about you? Now you have to walk back to your house on your own."

Nora's eyes glittered. "Yes. But no one messes with Precious."

Precious gave his best pit bull grin at Sam. Sam knew Precious was a sweetheart, but others would definitely think twice before tussling with Nora with Precious present.

Sam headed inside with Arlo, pouring him a bowl of fresh water and taking off all their winter outer layers.

She then went into her sunroom and looked at her list. Today was the day she'd wanted to go grocery shopping. She reviewed her list, which she'd made when she'd planned her menus for the week. Sam added a couple of dry goods to the list.

"I'm going to head out to the store," she told Arlo. "I'll be back in a little while, okay?"

Arlo gave her a doggy grin, then climbed into his dog bed, circling a few times before settling down with a happy sigh.

Sam walked out into the garage with her list and her purse. She spotted Chad's set of golf clubs there, leaning up against the wall, and sighed. That neighbor still hadn't come by to collect them and pay for them. Maybe she should list them again on a different online platform. She really didn't want to be confronted with any reminders of her ex-husband.

The store was quite hectic, and Sam frowned. Usually, it wasn't bad during the week. Then she remembered it was senior discount day. She usually avoided the store those days, but hadn't figured it into her plan for the week. Another indication that the murders had really knocked Sam off-schedule.

She navigated the crowded aisles and the long checkout lines as well as she could, then headed back to the house. There was something that was bothering her about the conversation she and Nora had earlier with Vanessa, but she couldn't put her finger on it. Her mind kept returning to Vanessa's outfit for some reason. Whatever it was, it was just slightly out of reach, which was frustrating. Sam decided to stop thinking about it, hoping maybe it would come to her.

She opened the garage with the remote and carefully pulled in. Then she got out of the car, opening the trunk to retrieve the groceries.

As Sam walked into the garage with a few bags of groceries, she couldn't shake the feeling that something was off. The hair on the back of her neck stood up, and she found herself scanning the shadows.

She shook her head, trying to dispel the unease. "You're being ridiculous," she muttered to herself. "It's broad daylight, for heaven's sake."

"Hello?" she called out, her voice sounding unnaturally loud in the enclosed space. "Is someone there?"

Silence.

Sam's heart was pounding now. She debated getting back in the car and driving away, but that felt like an overreaction. Instead, she reached into her purse, fingers closing around her keys. At least they could be used as a makeshift weapon if needed.

"I know someone's here," she said, trying to inject confidence into her voice. "Come out now, or I'm calling the police."

Which was when she heard a harsh voice coming out of the bushes.

Chapter Twenty-Five

"Sam," came Vanessa's voice from behind her. It wasn't a friendly greeting. It was cold, almost threatening.

Sam whirled around to see Vanessa standing there, a hoe that had been propped on the outside of the garage incongruously held in her hand. It made her look like a spectacularly dangerous farmer. She was wearing the same coat and beret from earlier. But now, the usually put-together woman looked wild-eyed and disheveled.

"Drop those bags. And those keys," ordered Vanessa in a clipped voice.

Reluctantly, Sam dropped them.

Sam cleared her throat and spoke, trying to keep her voice steady. "Your outfit. You wore the same thing to the dinner party."

"Yes, you mentioned that earlier. But it was cold, remember? And I went outside to take a business call."

Sam's voice was stronger now. "I'm not at all sure you were making a business call. I do believe you were out on the terrace, though. You'd have bundled up for that, for sure. When you went out there, were you just going to talk to Dom? Or had you already planned on getting rid of him then?"

"I don't know what you're talking about," said Vanessa in a flat voice.

"I think you do. If you're planning on killing me, there's no reason to keep things to yourself, is there? You've got to be proud of the way you've gotten away a murder and an attempted murder. You executed them well, didn't you?"

Vanessa gave a short laugh. "No pun intended? Sure, I think I did a good job. But then, I'm a pretty organized person, too. Not as organized as you, but then, who is? It's a shame your face is a dead giveaway. Can I ask *you* a question?"

Sam nodded.

"You obviously pegged me for this. How? Did you suddenly remember something from the party?"

Sam said, "Oh it was pretty serendipitous. When Arlo and I were heading out on our walk earlier, I happened into my neighbor. He swore a woman with black hair had been out on my terrace with Dom. He'd even told the police that. But, of course, none of the women at my dinner party had black hair. Or didn't seem to. When you're wearing your beret, you look like a brunette."

Sam's eyes darted around the garage, looking for an escape route, a weapon, anything. But Vanessa was between her and the safety of the outdoors. And Sam was always scrupulous about locking the door into the house from the garage.

"We can talk about this, Vanessa," Sam said, trying to keep her voice calm and reasonable. "Whatever happened, I'm sure there's an explanation."

Vanessa laughed, a harsh, brittle sound. "Oh, there's an explanation all right. But I'm afraid you won't be around to hear it."

"What's going on in here?" came Nora's imperious voice from behind them.

Vanessa whirled with a snarl, launching herself in Nora's direction. As Sam's survival instincts kicked in, in one fluid motion she grabbed a golf club from Chad's old set leaning against the wall and whacked it over Vanessa's head.

Nora and Sam stared down at Vanessa's still form. Arlo began barking wildly inside.

"Could you call the police, Nora?" asked Sam, her voice now definitely exhibiting the betraying tremor. "I'd better check for a pulse."

Fortunately, there was one, and Sam slumped in relief. Vanessa had been so very still. Nora's crisp voice brooked no argument as she told the police what had happened and to come immediately.

Sam held the golf club aloft, in case Vanessa did suddenly spring up from what seemed like a very deep state of unconsciousness. "What made you show up?" she asked Nora in a tired voice.

"The buddy system," said Nora curtly. "I was in my car, about to leave Maple Hills for that errand I was telling you about. I saw Vanessa, walking by herself down the street. I was going to give her a piece of my mind for not walking with a buddy. Then I noticed she was acting rather suspiciously. Especially when she settled into the bushes around your garage."

"Yes, that would seem a little suspicious," agreed Sam with a light laugh.

"Sadly, it took me quite a few minutes to walk up your driveway from the street. You do realize your driveway is quite steep." Nora sounded as if she were taking issue with the driveway, which had been in place at the historic home for many decades.

"Yes. Yes, it is. You didn't want to drive your car up?"

Nora gave her a look as if she strongly suspected she was an idiot. "Up this driveway? I'd never be able to turn around and get my vehicle back down again. No, I had to park in the street."

"Well, I'm really, really grateful you took the effort," said Sam warmly.

Nora gave the prone Vanessa a disdainful stare. "It was worth it. So she's the killer. She killed Dom and hurt Olivia."

The way Nora was pursing her lips, Sam was wondering if she was planning to spit on the unconscious Vanessa. "It certainly looks that way."

"But why?" demanded Nora. "Why would she do that?"

There was the faintest sound of a siren, quite far away.

"Let's ask her." Sam noticed Vanessa was stirring.

Chapter Twenty-Six

Sure enough, moments later, Vanessa was staring at Sam with unfocused eyes.

"I believe she has a concussion," said Nora with intense satisfaction.

Vanessa's gaze shifted in Nora's direction before she winced and closed her eyes again.

"We were wondering," said Sam politely, "if you could tell us why you murdered Dom and attacked Olivia. Just out of interest. The police are on their way, and you never got the chance to tell me how you'd been able to get away with the murder as long as you did."

Vanessa started to sit up, and Sam brandished the golf club at her. "Don't."

Vanessa cautiously lay back down on the cement floor of the garage again. "Okay." She groaned.

Nora snapped, "The murder and the attack. How and why."

Vanessa said, "Why do you think I'd tell you about that? Do you think I'm crazy? Why should I confess?"

"Yes, we do think you're crazy," said Nora. "But let's face the facts. There's no reason not to confess. You tried to kill Sam. I'm a witness. Let's start with Dom."

Vanessa said quietly, "Well, I had an affair with Dom."

"Tell me something I don't know. Although I don't know why you'd cheat on that nice Derek." Nora pursed her lips, looking judgmental.

"Because he's Nice Derek," said Vanessa slowly. "He's safe, intellectual, and boring. We also are having money problems. Dom was . . . volatile."

"Richer," said Nora with a sniff.

"Well, sure. I liked the presents he gave me. I thought I was a better match for him than Olivia was." Vanessa said Olivia's name as if she had nothing but contempt for her.

"What happened on the terrace?" asked Sam as the sirens approached.

Vanessa was quiet for a couple of moments, reflecting. "I went out to speak with Dom."

Nora snorted. "Dumb idea. That guy was in no condition to hold a reasonable conversation."

"Dom was drunk," said Vanessa. "But I thought I could use the opportunity to talk to him. He hadn't been answering my phone calls lately. I knew we'd have a private conversation, since no one else was going to hang out on the terrace. It was freezing out there."

Sam said, "And you'd been arguing over the phone and in-person. According to one witness, anyway."

Vanessa rolled her eyes. "Jason, of course. Yeah. Like I said, Dom was volatile. I wanted him to leave Olivia for me, and he said he was going to."

Nora snorted again. "Sure he was. That's one of the oldest lies around. You should know that."

Vanessa continued, as if Nora hadn't spoken. "Dom wasn't listening to me, though. He was being cruel. Brushing me off and laughing at me." Her face darkened. "I don't like being laughed at. So I reached out to push him. I was frustrated. I wasn't going to kill him."

"But you did," said Nora.

"He was already unsteady because of the drinking," said Vanessa. Her face was solemn. "I couldn't believe what had happened. I never meant Dom to be hurt. I cared about him."

"More fool you," said Nora.

"I was horrified," continued Vanessa. "I hurried away from the terrace."

Sam said, "But you were all bundled up in your winter clothes, including gloves. You needed a reason to have been outdoors in the frigid temperatures. A reason that didn't have anything to do with the terrace and Dom. So you stepped out for a phone call. Maybe you even told Derek you were going to return a phone call. Was Derek ever suspicious that you might have killed Dom?"

"Who knows?" said Vanessa with a short laugh. "I've never been able to figure out what goes through Derek's head. But he has been acting differently lately, so maybe so."

"And Olivia?" Nora demanded.

"She knew. She'd figured out I'd done it at some point after the party. I guess she saw me coming from the kitchen with my coat and hat on. I should never have put them on in the first place," said Vanessa.

The sirens were louder now.

"So you followed her," said Sam. "Maybe you drove over to her house with the hope of catching her alone, but Jason was there, going through Dom's things. Instead, you followed her car with your own. To the trail, intending to kill her."

Vanessa's voice was harsh, and she seemed to have a compunction to justify her actions. "Of course. I just told you that she knew. I went by her house with flowers Saturday morning, and I could see it in her eyes. Like I said, she must have remembered seeing me come in from the direction of the terrace."

"That makes sense. Spotting you coming in at the time wouldn't have really meant anything, would it? Olivia didn't realize Dom had died on the terrace steps because I hadn't gone out and discovered him yet. But Saturday morning, seeing you might have jarred something in her brain." Sam paused. "You also tried to invent another suspect by telling me Olivia was having an affair with someone. You were clearly hoping the mystery man would become a suspect."

Vanessa shrugged.

Nora said, "You besmirched Olivia's good name!"

Vanessa shrugged again.

The sirens blared as they headed up Sam's driveway with no issue at all. Vanessa slumped, an annoyed expression on her face. "Here comes the cavalry," she muttered.

Nora's face was blotchy with anger. "You tried to murder Olivia. In cold blood."

"And successfully murdered Dom," Sam commented.

"Who cares about Dom?" demanded Nora as the police approached.

And then, it was really all over. Lieutenant Phillips arrived with the uniformed police in tow.

"She did it!" said Nora, wildly pointing an arthritic finger at Vanessa. "And she was trying to kill Sam, too. See that hoe over there? She was going to hit Sam with it. She's the killer!"

Sam eventually gently led Nora inside to get a glass of iced tea. She'd gotten herself decidedly overwrought. Arlo, relieved to see Sam in one piece, trotted along with them. They settled into the sunroom, Nora still fuming, and waited for Phillips to read Vanessa her rights and lead her away for questioning at the station.

Then Phillips came in with a small notebook and asked if they were okay. His kindness prompted Nora to burst into tears, which startled both Phillips and Sam. Sam went in search of the tissue box, which was still in front of the fireplace from her conversation with a tearful Mandy.

Nora quickly regained control, unsurprisingly, and through gritted teeth, told Phillips exactly what she'd witnessed. Then she outlined precisely what Vanessa had owned up to. Phillips took notes before giving up and turning on his voice recorder. Nora, in her fury, was speaking entirely too fast for him to keep up.

Finally, Nora's monologue was complete, and Phillips turned to Sam. "Can you tell me how you figured out what happened? And how Vanessa realized you knew?"

Sam said, "Well, I spoke to my neighbor earlier. The birdwatcher."

Phillips's face looked wry, as if he might have thought the birdwatcher was also a keen observer of humans, too. "Right."

"He said he'd told the police about seeing a woman with black hair on the terrace with Dom. But, no one at the party had black hair."

Phillips nodded.

"So, probably like you, I dismissed what he'd said. It was dark, after all. How sure could he be of what he'd seen? But then, I came across Vanessa standing out in her yard a little while ago."

Nora broke in. "Smoking! She was smoking in her yard. I should have known right then she was the killer."

Sam continued. "Nora and her dog joined us for our walk."

Nora said, "Because of the buddy system. You shouldn't have been walking alone. Not with that smoking assassin on the loose."

Phillips's mouth was twitching as if it very much wanted to smile. He managed to control it, somehow. Nora wouldn't have appreciated any levity.

Sam said, "We spoke a few minutes with Vanessa. She was wearing the same black coat and matching black beret that she'd had on at my dinner party. I realized there was something about them that rang a bell with me. Vanessa must have seen that on my face, even if I didn't know exactly what I was remembering."

"What *were* you remembering?" asked Phillips.

"That she might have looked like she had black hair instead of blonde when she was wearing that beret. To the birdwatcher. So Vanessa decided, I guess to be on the safe side, that she needed to get rid of me."

"The very idea," said Nora scornfully.

"Then Nora appeared in the garage."

Phillips turned to Nora. "What made you arrive with such good timing?"

Nora sniffed. "The buddy system. I saw Vanessa out, *unaccompanied*, and hopped out to escort her before running my errand. But then I saw Vanessa was acting as if she were up to some sort of skullduggery. So I followed her."

"Thankfully," said Sam. "When Nora came in, she called out. Vanessa turned around. Then I put my ex-husband's golf club to good use."

Nora sniffed again. "It's the only good and generous thing Chad ever did."

Phillips turned off his voice recorder. "Well, you've both been a tremendous help."

"I should say we have," said Nora stiffly. "We solved your case for you. Now we can finally abandon the buddy system. If there's nothing else, I still have my errand to run."

Phillips quickly dismissed her, and Nora made her way carefully out the front door, then down the driveway to her car.

Sam felt the adrenaline from the confrontation with Vanessa ebb. She rubbed Arlo, who was sitting protectively in her lap. Phillips stood up. "Well, Ms. Prescott, I think we've covered everything for now. You've been through quite an ordeal." His voice was gruff but not unkind. "We'll be in touch if we need any further information. I'll head over to the hospital now and fill in Jason Barnes." As Phillips headed for the door, he turned back. "And Ms. Prescott? Try and get some rest. You're safe now."

The door clicked shut behind him. Sam glanced at the clock. The day had somehow both dragged on forever and shot by in a blur. She wanted to think that she could grab her book and fall asleep after thirty minutes of reading, Arlo on her lap. She'd like to be that person. But she knew herself too well. Even now, with the aforementioned adrenaline decreasing, she felt that restlessness that meant she needed to do something. One thing she needed to do was to bring the groceries inside. That little chore had certainly been delayed long enough.

After putting the groceries away, Sam said, "Arlo, let's head downstairs. Get a little exercise in."

Arlo looked at Sam as if he'd already gotten his exercise in with the walk with Nora and Precious earlier. But he amiably followed her as she changed into exercise clothes, then trotted downstairs behind Sam, watching with interest as she proceeded to do both strength training and cardio.

Finally, after the exercise and a shower afterwards, Sam felt less keyed-up. The hot water had washed away some of the tension, leaving her muscles pleasantly sore. She padded into the kitchen, her damp hair leaving a trail of droplets on her shoulders. As she reached for a granola bar, her stomach growled, reminding her she hadn't eaten since . . . when? The day's events had blurred together.

Sam's phone rang abruptly. Seeing Jason's name, she was instantly alert. "Jason? Everything okay?"

"She's awake." His voice was thick with emotion. "They started reducing the sedation this morning, and she opened her eyes about an hour ago. She's groggy." He gave a shaky laugh. "But she knew who I was, Sam. She squeezed my hand."

Sam pressed a hand to her chest, feeling tears spring to her eyes. "That's wonderful news. Has she said anything?"

"Not really talking yet; the doctors say that's normal. They're running tests, checking her responses." His voice dropped lower. "The police are already here. Phillips told me everything. I'm so glad you got away from Vanessa. This whole thing has just been so crazy. But now it's going to be over. The cops said as soon as Olivia's able to communicate clearly, they want to question her."

"Which will give the police even more evidence against Vanessa."

"Yeah." Jason paused. "Listen, I've got to go—the neurologist is here. Thanks for everything, Sam."

After they hung up, Sam sat quietly for a moment, processing everything that had happened. The day had been a whirlwind—from the terrifying confrontation with Vanessa in her garage to the news of Olivia waking up. She wasn't sure whether to feel relieved, exhausted, or both.

Just then, there was a gentle knock on her door. Arlo's ears perked up, his head tilting in that adorable way that always made Sam smile. He didn't bark, which was a good sign. When Sam opened the door, Aiden was standing there, concern etched on his face. The late afternoon sun caught his hair, giving him a soft glow that made Sam's breath catch for a moment.

"Hey," he said softly, "I heard what happened. I wanted to check on you."

"Come on in," said Sam, stepping aside. She felt a wave of relief wash over her, not realizing until that moment how much she'd needed to see a friendly face.

They settled on the sofa in the sunroom, the golden light filtering through the windows, casting long shadows across the room. Arlo, ever the opportunist, happily wedged himself between them, his tail thumping against the cushions.

"How are you holding up?" asked Aiden, his eyes searching her face.

Sam let out a shaky laugh, running her fingers through her damp hair. "Honestly, I'm not sure. It still feels a little surreal. Did Vanessa really come over to my house and try to kill me?" She shook her head, the reality of the situation hitting her anew. "But yeah, I'm doing all right, I guess. I worked out this afternoon for a while, and it helped me feel less jittery. Though I think I might have overdone it a bit on the treadmill."

"I think the jitters are completely normal, after what happened," Aiden reassured her, his hand unconsciously moving to pat Arlo. "I found out what happened right after school let out. The news spread like wildfire through the faculty room."

Sam's eyes opened wide. She'd momentarily forgotten about Derek. Had the police called him out of his classroom to tell him the news about his wife being arrested? "How's Derek doing?" she asked.

Aiden's expression turned somber. "He's struggling. Finding out your wife is a murderer isn't exactly anything you can prepare for. Derek's sister is coming over to stay with him for a while to help him out so he can process everything. He looked shell-shocked when I saw him. Like he couldn't quite believe it was real."

"I'm glad he's got family coming over." Sam made a face, memories of her own ordeal with Chad flooding back. "I've been through the same thing, you know, with Chad. It'll take some time. I'll let Derek know I can be an ear if he wants to talk it through with someone. Sometimes it helps to unload to someone who's been there."

They sat in companionable silence for a moment.

"You know," Aiden said finally, his voice soft, almost hesitant, "I think it was really great you had that dinner party, even after everything you'd been through with Chad. It was brave of you, doing something like that. I'm sorry it ended up the way it did."

Sam smiled at him. "Thanks, Aiden. That means a lot."

He reached out, gently squeezing her hand before letting it go again. The brief contact sent a tingle up Sam's arm. "I hope things start looking up for you soon. You deserve it. You've been through more than your fair share of drama."

Sam took a deep breath, squaring her shoulders. "You know what? I'm going to do it again."

Aiden raised an eyebrow, a mix of surprise and admiration on his face. "Another dinner party?"

"Yep," Sam said, a determined glint in her eye. "But this time, for the agility club. Laid-back. No murder mysteries, just good food and dog talk. And you should come, too. You might enjoy meeting these guys."

Aiden's face broke into a grin, his eyes crinkling at the corners. "Now that sounds like a plan I can get behind."

Two weeks later, Sam stood in her kitchen, a sense of déjà vu washing over her. But this time, instead of anxiety, she felt a bubbling excitement. The counters were laden with appetizers, the smell of chicken filled the air, and a stack of brightly colored dog bowls sat ready by the back door.

"Okay, Arlo," she said, looking down at her furry companion, "what do you think? Chicken kabobs for the humans, and these gourmet dog biscuits for our four-legged friends?"

Arlo's tail wagged enthusiastically, thumping against the kitchen tiles. He gave a soft "woof" of approval.

The doorbell rang, its chime mixing with the sound of excited barking from outside. Sam smoothed down her apron, took a deep breath, and felt a smile spread across her face. "Here we go, buddy."

She opened the door to find Ginny, Dave, Lucy, Melissa, and their dogs, all wearing party hats that looked in danger of being thrown off at any second. The dogs were practically vibrating with excitement, their leashes tangled as they tried to sniff everything at once.

"Let the puppy party begin!" Ginny exclaimed, her enthusiasm infectious. Her wild red curls were barely contained by her own party hat, giving her the appearance of a particularly festive lion.

As Sam ushered them in, laughing as the dogs immediately began a thorough inspection of her foyer, she caught sight of Aiden walking up her driveway. He was carrying a bottle of wine in one hand and a bag of dog toys in the other, and the sight of him made her heart skip a beat.

"Room for one more?" he called out, a warm smile on his face.

Sam felt her heart lift. "Always," she replied, holding the door open wider.

About the Author

B estselling cozy mystery author Elizabeth Spann Craig is a
library-loving, avid mystery reader. A pet-owning South-
erner, her four series are full of cats, corgis, and cheese grits. The
mother of two, she lives with her husband, a fun-loving corgi,
and a couple of cute cats.

Sign up for Elizabeth's free newsletter to stay updated on re-
leases:

https://bit.ly/2xZUXqO

This and That

I love hearing from my readers. You can find me on Facebook as Elizabeth Spann Craig Author, on Twitter as elizabeth-scraig, on my website at elizabethspanncraig.com, and by email at elizabethspanncraig@gmail.com.

Thanks so much for reading my book...I appreciate it. If you enjoyed the story, would you please leave a short review on the site where you purchased it? Just a few words would be great. Not only do I feel encouraged reading them, but they also help other readers discover my books. Thank you!

Did you know my books are available in print and ebook formats? Most of the Myrtle Clover series is available in audio and some of the Southern Quilting mysteries are. Find the audiobooks here: https://elizabethspanncraig.com/audio/

Please follow me on BookBub for my reading recommendations and release notifications.

I'd also like to thank some folks who helped me put this book together. Thanks to my cover designer, Karri Klawiter, for her awesome covers. Thanks to my editor, Judy Beatty for her help. Thanks to beta readers Amanda Arrieta, Rebecca Wahr, Cassie Kelley, and Dan Harris for all of their helpful suggestions and careful reading. Thanks to my ARC readers for helping to spread the word. Thanks, as always, to my family and readers.

Other Works by Elizabeth

Myrtle Clover Series in Order (be sure to look for the Myrtle series in audio, ebook, and print):

Pretty is as Pretty Dies

Progressive Dinner Deadly

A Dyeing Shame

A Body in the Backyard

Death at a Drop-In

A Body at Book Club

Death Pays a Visit

A Body at Bunco

Murder on Opening Night

Cruising for Murder

Cooking is Murder

A Body in the Trunk

Cleaning is Murder

Edit to Death

Hushed Up

A Body in the Attic

Murder on the Ballot

Death of a Suitor

A Dash of Murder

Death at a Diner

A Myrtle Clover Christmas

Murder at a Yard Sale

Doom and Bloom

A Toast to Murder

Mystery Loves Company (2025)

THE VILLAGE LIBRARY Mysteries in Order:

Checked Out

Overdue

Borrowed Time

Hush-Hush

Where There's a Will

Frictional Characters

Spine Tingling

A Novel Idea

End of Story

Booked Up

Out of Circulation

Shelf Life (2025)

The Sunset Ridge Mysteries in Order

The Type-A Guide to Solving Murder

The Type-A Guide to Dinner Parties (2025)

Southern Quilting Mysteries in Order:

Quilt or Innocence

Knot What it Seams

Quilt Trip
Shear Trouble
Tying the Knot
Patch of Trouble
Fall to Pieces
Rest in Pieces
On Pins and Needles
Fit to be Tied
Embroidering the Truth
Knot a Clue
Quilt-Ridden
Needled to Death
A Notion to Murder
Crosspatch
Behind the Seams
Quilt Complex
A Southern Quilting Cozy Christmas

MEMPHIS BARBEQUE MYSTERIES in Order (Written as Riley Adams):

Delicious and Suspicious
Finger Lickin' Dead
Hickory Smoked Homicide
Rubbed Out

And a standalone "cozy zombie" novel: Race to Refuge, written as Liz Craig

Printed in the USA
CPSIA information can be obtained
at www.ICGtesting.com
LVHW010315161124
796761LV00001B/10